DEAD AIM

Lund Taylor heard the horses but his reflex action was directed at Lee Morgan. He fired. He probably heard the two shots, which were fired almost at the same time behind him. It was less likely that he felt them, although both hit home. Lund Taylor was dead before he hit the ground.

Taylor's shot at Morgan had been just a fraction of an inch too high. It took Morgan's hat off but the agile gunman had dropped to one knee, drawing at the same time. His skills, both inherent and practiced, once again paid dividends. Both riders tumbled from their saddles.

Also in the *Buckskin* Series:

BUCKSKIN #19

SHOTGUN STATION

KIT DALTON

LEISURE BOOKS   NEW YORK CITY

A LEISURE BOOK®

October 2004

Published by

Dorchester Publishing Co., Inc.
200 Madison Avenue
New York, NY 10016

ISBN 0-8439-2529-9

Visit us on the web at www.dorchesterpub.com.

BUCKSKIN #19

SHOTGUN STATION

1

Lee Morgan had been riding, sun up to sundown, for the past ten days. He'd ridden into Texas on the fifteenth day of April, somewhere up in the panhandle. He was still in Texas and he was still a half a day's ride from his destination.

He'd bedded down with a whore named Daisy up in Amarillo. He'd lost more than he could afford in a poker game in Lubbock. A drunk half breed Apache had tried to give him a haircut in Big Spring and he heard about a job that nobody else wanted when he passed through San Angelo. He was headed for Uvalde and hating Texas more with each mile.

Uvalde was on the sun up side of the Anacacho mountain range. By Morgan's reckoning, some sixty miles from the Mexican border. The populace was two thirds Mexican with the balance made up of a mixed breed of Mexican, Indian and drifter. By the time he rode into town, he'd already decided that none of it would be worth saving should the need ever arise.

"Stall him, water him, feed him and after he's cooled down pull the burrs out of his legs and rub them down with linament."

"Si señor," the livery man replied. Simultaneously, grinning a toothless grin, he held up two short, dirty fingers. "Two pesos now an' two pesos *manana."* Morgan frowned. "You will come then to see me. If you are not happy," the man continued, glancing at Morgan's blacksnake whip, "who knows what you will do, *señor.* It is a *jugar."* The man shrugged. "A gamble, *señor."*

"Yeah. And if I *am* happy?"

"Two pesos more—and he stays for as long as you like."

Morgan eyed the man. Sweat trickled from his forehead in a steady stream and finally dispersed into a number of wrinkles on his chubby, jowled face. He was balding, squinty eyed and part of his left ear was missing. His shoulders were round and held up big, powerful-looking arms. The rest of him was lard covered with coarse, black hair. He wore outsized, home sewn, denim britches. They were held up with overburdened galluses stained with sweat. He had no shirt and on his feet only sandals.

Morgan dug into his pockets and came up with four dollars. He grabbed the man's wrist, pulled his arm down and pressed the money into a sweaty palm. The man looked shocked. "All of it right now," Morgan said, "and I *will* be back tomorrow. If I'm *not* happy, you lose the *jugar."* Their eyes met. Both then smiled and the livery man nodded, jerking free and jamming the money into his pants pocket. Morgan noted the strain the action placed on the galluses. "One more thing, *amigo*—a hotel. Uvalde got one?"

"Si, señor." He took Morgan by the upper part of his arm and led him just outside the livery barn. There, he

freed his grip and pointed toward the tallest building in sight. "The hotel—she is there." The man turned his head, looked Morgan in the eye, grinned broadly and added, *"La cucaracha!"*

The man at the livery barn hadn't lied. At least not about the cockroaches. Morgan knew he wouldn't be alone in his room. After dispatching the most daring of the disgusting insects, Morgan stripped and washed off as much of Texas as the facilities allowed. That done, he broke out his only change of clothes, dressed, strapped on his rig and went downstairs to the *cantina*. He was gratified to find an American barkeep.

"We got ice," the man said proudly. "Want a cold beer, mister?"

"Yeah." Morgan had expected a mug of beer with ice in it. The practice was common in most places if they were fortunate enough to have ice at all. Here, he found himself the recipient of a frost coated mug and beer from a keg which was surrounded by ice. It was delicious. He drank two before he spoke again.

"You want another beer, mister?"

Morgan nodded and then asked, "Where would I find Luke Masters?"

"Prob'ly down to his office." The barkeep set up the beer and then eyed Morgan. "You his new shotgun rider?"

"Word travels fast."

"Easy to figure. You don't look like a man with freight to haul and there ain't nobody else lookin' for Luke Masters 'cept for that job. Three's come in askin —an' three's rode out right after."

"Hard man to work for?"

The barkeep grinned. "Luke? Hell no. Got a disposition like a pup's—ceptin' maybe where his daughter is concerned. Mostly, though—shotgun men ridin' for Luke Masters got a mighty short life span lately."

"Know why?"

"Sure don't. Nobody else can figure it either. Up 'til about six months ago, Luke had only been robbed one time. Now all o' the sudden, his wagons been hit about a dozen times. He's lost four shotgun men an' two damn good skinners."

"Well," Morgan said, finishing his beer, "I'm not looking to end up at my own funeral but I heard the pay was pretty good."

" 'Bout the best in these parts if you live to spend it."

As Morgan took his leave, he brushed by two cowhands just coming in. One of them paused and eyed him closely. Morgan returned the stare until the cowpoke finally turned away. It appeared to Morgan that the man thought he recognized him. Morgan knew he had never seen the cowhand. It puzzled him.

The Masters' Cartage Company was housed in one of the more attractive of Uvalde's buildings. In part, that could be attributed to sharing some office space with Wells-Fargo & Co. The stage line had bought out two local firms about four years earlier and now maintained the only stage line to points west and south of Uvalde. While the railroads had forced Wells-Fargo to shrink its passenger hauling duties up north, rail transport in Texas was still begging.

The bell over the office door rang twice. Once when Morgan opened the door and again when he closed it. Neither brought anyone to the desk. Morgan's eyes scanned the photographs on the walls. Most, he .reckoned, were twenty-five or thirty years old. Luke

Masters' father had founded the company and had hauled freight for some prominent clients. Among the pictures, Morgan recognized Kit Carson, Temple Houston—son of the Texas legend Sam Houston, and the fabled New Mexico lawman Pat Garrett.

"May I help you?" Morgan's head jerked toward the desk. The voice was soft—like velvet but somewhat throaty. Morgan's eyes fell upon a blonde haired, blue eyed beauty who, he guessed, was probably about twenty-five. Her hair was short and tucked up under a stetson. She wore a tight fitted buckskin shirt and britches which seemed molded to her form.

"Maybe," he said. "I'm looking for Luke Masters. I'm here about a job." The girl eyed him.

"You're no skinner."

"You're right. I sent a telegraph cable. Name's Lee Morgan."

"The shotgun." Morgan nodded. The girl came from behind the desk and extended her hand. The grip was firm. "I'm Lucy Masters. I run the office and do most of the hiring. My father is at the bank right now but you'd end up talking to me first anyhow."

"Your daddy don't make the decisions?"

"We make them together. I'm a full partner."

"The pay sounded pretty good," Morgan said, tentatively.

"It's very good but you'll earn every dime of it. We've been hit on seventeen of the last twenty-five runs. We're down to two skinners and no shotguns. You'll get expenses when you're not in Uvalde. A hundred and fifty a month wages. All the ammunition you use on the job and a bonus for every shipment that gets through." She smiled. "That's payable twice a year if you're still around to collect it."

"None of it sounds negotiable."

"None of it is."

"Maybe that's why you don't have any shotgun riders."

"No maybe about it. That's the reason, Mr. Morgan, and that's the way it stays. Take it or leave it."

"Then I'm hired," he said, adding, "*if* I take it?"

"I didn't say that. I just said that those are the rules. If you can't abide them, then there's no need to waste any more time—yours or mine."

"I can live with 'em, but I'd like to know who's out to get you."

"So would we."

"Any ideas?"

"None that I care to discuss with you, Mr. Morgan." She smiled and cocked her head. "At least not right now." She turned on her heel and went back behind the desk. She turned back. "A drink?"

"Whiskey." She poured. Morgan downed the shot and she offered another. He declined. "You said you had two drivers. They both new?"

"Only one. Sam Tanksley. He's from Amarillo. Skinned for Wells-Fargo awhile back. Comes well spoke of. Our other man has been with daddy for ten years." She grinned and shook her head. "If he was fifteen years younger we wouldn't need you. He could do both."

"Sounds like quite a man."

"He is. His name is Cimmaron Dakis but we—matter of fact most—just call him Alkali."

"I'd guess there's a story behind that," Morgan said, smiling.

"There is, but don't ask him to tell it when I'm

12

around. I've heard it more than my share."

The door opened and Morgan turned to see a well dressed, big man of about fifty. He had a leathery face and a friendly smile. Morgan guessed right when he concluded that the man was Luke Masters. After the proper introductions, Lucy Masters returned to her work on the company books. Morgan and the elder Masters spent more than an hour together. The conversation concluded with Masters' invite for Morgan to join them that evening for dinner. It would officially seal their bargain. Too, Masters invited Morgan to stay at the Masters' home so long as he was in their employ. It was not a practice Morgan usually indulged but two things were gnawing at him. The first was the mystery of the sudden raids on Masters' freight wagons. The second could be found at the hotel—*La Cucaracha!*

2

The Double C cattle ranch stretched out over thousands of acres of southwest Texas grassland. The main house and the center of the Double C's activities was located just a dozen miles southeast of Uvalde. West and south of the house, all the way to the Mexican border at Piedras Negras and south along the Rio Grande, Double C cattle were fattened up.

The ranch was nearly as much a part of Texas as the Alamo. Founded by Trevor and Ephram Coltrane in 1837, the operation came into its own under Trevor's son, Houston. At the birth of his daughter, Houston Coltrane lost his wife. He threw himself into raising her and expanding his empire. He did so, finally, to the exclusion of his illegitimate son, Marshall.

The day Marsh Coltrane was run off was a day still talked about in that part of Texas. Marsh decided he was man enough to handle his daddy. He was wrong. Whipped and humiliated, Marsh rode off and out of Houston Coltrane's will. He swore revenge. Three years later, the old man died and left everything to his legitimate heir, Charity Coltrane.

Charity was twenty-eight, nearly six feet tall, almond-eyed, dark of complexion and full bosomed. She could turn any man's head, dance with the best of Texas' wealthy ladies and outshoot most of the ranch hands. Save for social events, Charity Coltrane would be in denim pants, wool shirt, chaps, dogging boots and toting a pair of matched Colt's pistols. They weren't just for show.

She knew most of the Double C's ranch hands by their first names, except during the spring drives which she headed up. Once the drive was over, she turned her attention to the second of the ranch's income producing ventures—horses. Charity Coltrane could break, ride, brand and deal on cattle or horse flesh with a skill envied by the most case hardened buyer. In short, she was a woman with whom to be reckoned.

Lige Brewster, one of the ranch's top hands, pounded on the front door of the main house. The West Indian black, Kingston, responded.

"Need to see Miss Charity," Lige said, sheepishly, Kingston stepped back, eyed the hand's dirty boots and then pointed to a small rug at one side of the entryway. Lige nodded and stood on it. A few minutes later, Charity Coltrane appeared from the den.

"What is it, Lige?"

"Not real sure ma'am—but—well—I think I saw your bro—" He stopped. It was the wrong thing to call Marsh Coltrane—if it had been Marsh Coltrane he saw. Lige cleared his throat. "I think I saw Marsh Coltrane ma'am—yestiddy—at the hotel casino."

"Lige, you weren't around when Marsh was here. How can you say that?"

"I—I seen his picture, ma'am." He paused, pointing

toward the den, then he continued. "Used to hang in there—behind your poppa's desk."

Charity walked over to him. "That would take some remembering on your part."

"Yes'm—an' I said—I'm not positive but you allus tol' us—if'n we think we seen 'im—we was s'posed to say."

Charity considered him. Finally, she nodded. "Yes Lige, yes I did." She squeezed her temples between her thumb and two fingers and turned away, walking several steps before she turned back. "You fetch Li Sung and take him to town. He near raised Marsh Coltrane. If anybody would recognize him Li Sung would." Lige Brewster looked surprised. "Ma'am—I figured *you*—"

"I'll do the figuring Lige—not you. Just do what I've asked." She smiled. An order out of Charity Coltrane was never an order. Lige nodded. "When you get back send the Chinese to see me."

Lee Morgan found himself awakened to a tray of orange juice fresh squeezed, flapjacks, eggs, bacon and a pot of coffee. Lucy Masters served it up personally.

"If you'll forgive me saying so," Morgan offered, scooting up to a sitting position, "this is a hell of a way to treat a hired hand."

"Enjoy it today, Mr. Morgan. It won't happen again." She placed the tray and poured the coffee. Morgan was pleased when she produced a second empty cup and poured herself a cup. She wasn't bashful. She sat down on the edge of the bed. "Daddy likes you." They both sipped and eyed each other. "He told me you were the offspring of a pretty famous old gunman."

"Frank Leslie got around."

"Or his reputation did."

"Hmm!"

"You as good as he was supposed to be?"

Morgan chewed, swallowed and followed the mouthful with a swallow of coffee. "He wasn't *supposed* to be anything. He *was* something. I'm something too—me—Lee Morgan. I'm not Buckskin Frank Leslie."

"You sound a little resentful."

"Only of the fact that I prefer to be judged by what I do. Not who fate happened to make me."

"Fair enough." Lucy Masters poured both of them a second cup of coffee. Then, she got up and walked across the room, finally turning back. Morgan had been watching her. "You'll have a chance to prove just how good you are, Mr. Morgan. We're sending you to San Antonio to negotiate a new contract for us."

Morgan stopped eating. He considered Lucy's statement and searched her face for any sign of a joke. There was none.

"Why me? I thought I was hired on as a shotgun rider."

"You were—but if we don't land this contract—we'll have very little need of your services. Most of our clientele have either already quit us or cut down their shipments until it is difficult to make the runs pay."

"Still—why me? I'd think you or your daddy would want to handle a contract personally just to make sure you've got a more than even chance to get it."

"Usually that would be the case. On this one—well—I've got some questions about it. You're the kind of man who is supposed to be able to get the answers." She took several short sips of coffee. "Have you ever heard of Jesus Benitalde Sanchez de Lopez?''

Morgan was finishing his breakfast. He didn't answer until he was through. He eyed the girl and decided to test her mettle even further. He swung his legs from beneath the covers. She didn't even blink. He stood up, glancing back at her. Her eyes roamed over his muscular frame but she made no effort to turn away. Morgan began to dress.

"I've heard of him. Stories in the newspapers mostly." Morgan began tucking in his shirt. "Seems I recall something about a revolution."

"Uh huh—and we don't want to be mixed up in any revolution." Morgan sat on the edge of the bed and tugged on his boots. He stood up, reached for his rig and strapped it on.

"But you want the business—and the uh—*pesos* that go with it."

"That's not a *want,* Mr. Morgan. That's a *need.*"

"If you're going to dig in the dirt for your gold, Miss Masters, you're going to get your hands dirty."

She snickered. "Son of a famous gunman—no slouch himself and a philosopher in the boot. Well then, Mr. Morgan, you have a looksee at the Lopez deal and you decide just how dirty our hands are going to get."

"You still haven't answered my questions. Why me?"

"Protocol, Mr. Morgan," Lucy snapped. "Great men rarely meet face to face to negotiate." She smiled. "They dispatch emissaries."

Lee Morgan had been a lot of things in his life. He could not recall ever having been an emissary. The word grated on him. He concluded that what it really meant was simply that he was expendable. As a shotgun rider

—the same was true. Thing was, as a shotgun rider he could shoot back. Frankly, Morgan didn't know what to expect as an emissary.

Morgan was to ride out that afternoon. About noon, he left the freight office and headed for the livery barn. Half way there, he noted the cowpoke who'd stared at him as he was leaving the hotel on his first day in town. The cowpoke was in company with a Chinese man. This time they were both staring.

Morgan could feel their eyes upon him even after he'd passed them. Finally, he stopped and turned around. They were still staring but the Chinese got nervous, shook his head up and down and then turned and trotted off. The cowpoke looked back at Morgan and then he too turned and walked away. Morgan vowed, silently, that he would confront the cowpoke if he ever saw him again.

Li Sung bowed low as he entered the Double C ranch house. He stood, head bowed, while Kingston fetched the lady of the house. Charity Coltrane ushered Li Sung into the den and closed the door behind them.

"Li Sung—is Marshall in Uvalde?"

"It is many years, Missy. Li Sung's eyes not so good."

"Is it," she repeated, her voice more harsh the second time.

"I thinkee so. I thinkee master Marsh back—yes—yes."

Ten years could make quite a difference in anyone's appearance. In the case of the Coltrane clan, it was even more. Charity had gone off to a girl's school in Dallas when she was twelve. Aside from holidays and a rare visit from her father and stepbrother, she rarely saw anyone from the Double C. She had no more than returned home when the final split took place. Once that happened, her father removed all evidence of Marshall Coltrane's existence.

It had been difficult for Charity to understand how her father could have so completely reversed himself about Marsh. Once, he had done little but brag about the boy. The son he'd fathered in a single moment of passionate indiscretion. What had happened? Charity really never knew the details but the hatred between the two, or so she believed, was a major contributing factor to her father's premature death. As for Marsh, he made no secret of his intent to avenge his exile.

Charity rode, hell bent, into Uvalde and sought out Sheriff Lund Taylor. He was a big, slow, affable man who could be seen patrolling the streets with a shotgun in one hand and an axe handle in the other. Charity couldn't recall ever having heard of Lund Taylor shooting anybody.

"Miss Charity, you're a sight for sore eyes. Don't see near enough o' you these days." The sheriff had lifted his 225-pound frame out of the broken-down chair behind his desk. He stood, rather in a slouch, grinning down at Charity. He was nearly six feet, six inches tall.

"I have reason to believe that Marshall has come back. I want to know what you intend to do about it if it's true."

Lund Taylor straightened up and walked around the desk. He seated himself on its edge and then folded his arms across his chest.

"He done somethin' wrong?"

"You *know* what he did."

The sheriff was already shaking his head negatively. "No, Miss Charity," Lund said, holding up his right hand and extending his index finger into the air, "I know what he said. They's a difference. Stiil cain't jail a man fer talkin'."

"I've seen you pole ax a man for damn little more than just thinking."

"Yes'm. Drunk cowhands talkin' wild. Boys, most of 'em, mean no harm. Too much bad whiskey an' too long on the trail. I do that mostly fer the ramrods. They sleep it off and they's fine the next mornin'. Now, ma'am, you 're talkin' 'bout somethin' a whole heap differ'nt."

"What's he have to do? Burn down the Double C?"

Sheriff Lund Taylor grinned. "Ma'am, they ain't a man in a hunnert miles could do that. Why your boys'd have 'im strung up to a willow branch before he could git inside o' five miles from the house."

"I came here to get the law where it belongs—on my side." Charity's dark eyes flashed and she spun around, strode to the door and then turned back. "You've been *informed,* Sheriff. Anything that happens now is self defense."

"Miss Charity, the law works in both directions. Just you make sure, if anythin' does happen, that you're defendin' and not agaitatin'." The sheriff smiled and then added, "But I'll ask around. If'n it turns out to be Marsh, I'll have a little talk with 'im."

"Marsh Coltrane won't be coming back here to *talk,* Sheriff. Not even to you."

Charity was just mounting up when a feminine voice called to her. She turned and saw Lucy Masters approaching. The two of them represented about the most desirable, if not available, female element in Uvalde. Between them there was no love lost. Upon the Masters' arrival in Uvalde, Lucy's father had quickly sized up the Coltrane ranch as a likely freight customer. Charity was on a trip to the east at the time, however. By the time she returned, Lucy had replaced her as a young cowhand's favorite. Ultimately, Jack Henshaw rode out of their lives but no business dealings ever culminated between the two.

"Miss Masters," Charity said, coolly, as Lucy approached.

"I'll be both frank and brief," Lucy said. "We've been robbed a number of times lately and I've heard rumors that your own ranch has also been a target. I know your present freight arrangements are costly and we need your business. Do you still think Jack Henshaw is worth it?"

Charity considered Lucy for several seconds, mentally evaluating the assessments to which she had just alluded. Finally, Charity smiled.

"No," she said. "I don't. What do you propose?"

"A re-evaluation of our positions—a consideration of busineess between us. I'd suggest that my father come to your ranch at your convenience and discuss it."

"Very well," Charity said. "I've had some, uh, personal news with which I must deal right now. Shall we say one day next week."

"You name it."

"I'll send word to you." Lucy nodded. Just inside the office, Sheriff Lund watched the meeting with interest and concern. He had a healthy respect for most men he might have to face down. He got a cold chill down his spine when he pondered the possibilities of having to face either one or both of the hellcats he'd just been watching.

3

Morgan reined up, removed his hat and mopped his brow. He eyed a half dozen citizens who, like himself, had paused in front of the old mission called the Alamo. After a few minutes of remembering his history and mentally reciting a part of the roster of names, Morgan knew that here was Texas and here too—America. He rode on, turning onto Commerce and riding, once again, outside the city boundaries.

The Mexican *hacienda* architecture clearly marked the residence of Jesus Benitalde Sanchez de Lopez. Two sombreroed *vaqueros* stood vigil at the arched entry way. Above it, fashioned in black wrought iron were the words

La Casa de Lopez

"Pararse!" Morgan halted. *"Que habla Espanol?"*

"Some," Morgan replied, smiling and then adding, *"Poco."*

"Como se llama?" The tallest of the *vaqueros* stepped forward as he spoke. *"Nombre?"*

"Morgan. Lee Morgan. I have come to see *Señor* de Lopez. I come from *Señorita* Masters in Uvalde."

"*Esperar.*" Morgan dismounted to wait. A few minutes later, he was escorted into the house. Its interior was plush, resplendent with the trappings of success. In what was obviously the library, Morgan was given a drink and told to make himself comfortable. A few minutes later, he turned toward the sound of the opening door and saw a tall, slim, well groomed middle aged man.

"*Señor* Morgan, I am Jesus de Lopez." The man approached, shook Morgan's hand and gestured toward a nearby overstuffed chair. Morgan got comfortable. "May I refresh your drink?"

"Yeah—uh—yes," Morgan said, "thank you."

"Now then, *señor,* I was given to understand that the Masters family harbored some reservations about contracting with us. Is that correct?"

"I think they have some questions."

"And you were sent to get the answers." The man smiled. "You look more like a *pistolero* than a businessman."

"Different business requires different skills."

"Agreed, Mr. Morgan. Some of my business requires men of your particular skill." Lopez turned toward the door. "Enrique!" Morgan looked up and a sinister looking man entered. He wore crossed *bandoleros* each of which supported a pistol. Morgan eased to his feet. Lopez turned back, smiling at Morgan. "Now," Lopez said.

Morgan's right hand became a blur but the barrel of his gun was leveled not at Enrique but squarely between

Lopez's eyes. Enrique's own guns were not yet in position.

"I don't like games," Morgan said.

"I'm impressed, Mr. Morgan. Enrique is one of my best men. Obviously you could have killed him easily." Lopez frowned. "Instead you chose me as your target."

"I doubt that I could get out of here alive," Morgan said, "even if I killed your man. I'd rather reduce the incentive than try to reduce the odds."

"I had to know just how good you are," Lopez said, extending his hands, palms upward and shrugging. "I hope you understand."

"I understand. But you still don't know, Lopez. I would have killed both of you." Enrique frowned and took a step forward. Lopez held up his hand.

"I think you could have, Mr. Morgan. Enrique, *vamos.*" The sinister *vaquero* took his leave but his eyes never strayed from Morgan's face. Morgan holstered his gun, finished his drink and sat down. This time, however, he did not lean back. Instead, he leaned forward.

"What's your deal?"

"Will you accept my hospitality for the evening, Mr. Morgan? Dinner with myself and my family? A tour of the grounds later perhaps? A good night's rest? I much prefer business talk at the start of the day. Too," Lopez said, smiling, "I would consider it a way of apologizing to you."

"I'll accept," Morgan said, "on one condition."

"Yes."

"No more games. The next man of yours who pulls a gun on me is going to die. Understood?"

"Understood," Lopez said.

Morgan's tour of the house served little more than to substantiate what he already knew. Jesus de Lopez was a wealthy man. A tour of the grounds was another matter. Once a visitor left the immediate environs of the house, the property became a compound. Morgan reckoned that more than a hundred *vaqueros* were bivouacked on the premises and there was no doubt facilities for twice that number.

"I'm impressed," Morgan said, adding, "as I assume I'm supposed to be." Lopez grinned.

"That you are is complimentary but I doubt that you have been swayed even minimally in your thinking."

"I wouldn't go quite that far," Morgan replied. "A gang of men like you've got quartered here could raise hell with hit and run raids." He considered Lopez, smiled and said, "Couldn't they?"

"They could—but they haven't. Not yet anyway."

"Revolution, *señor* Lopez? I've heard stories."

"I've heard the same ones but I too own a cattle ranch. It is, by Texas standards, rather modest but it does require *vaqueros.*"

"Yeah—sure."

Two chairs were still vacant at the dining room table when Morgan joined Lopez, Juan Diaz—Lopez's foreman, and a Mexican banker introduced as Francisco Correra. A few minutes after the formal introductions, one of the chairs was filled. Morgan could not hide his appetite.

"This is my daughter, Mr. Morgan. Madiera, come meet the *rayo veloz yanqui.*" Morgan looked quizzical. Madiera Lucia de Lopez extended her hand, backside up in anticipation of it being kissed. Morgan shook it.

"I am pleased," she said, smiling. "My father called you a lightning-fast yankee. I assume he refers to your skill with a weapon."

"It's all he's seen," Morgan said. "And meeting you is my pleasure."

"Gracias, señor."

"Bien venido, señorita."

The sixth chair at the table remained empty throughout the meal though a place had been set. Morgan glanced at it and then at Jesus de Lopez several times. He got no indication that things were not as they should be. The talk remained small. Mostly about horses, cattle and the stunning growth of Texas during the past century.

"Tell me, Morgan," de Lopez finally said, wiping the corners of his mouth as he finished his meal, "how do you perceive the acquisition of Texas by the United States?"

"If they stole it they stole too much. If they didn't they could have afforded to be generous and taken less." The reply brought laughter.

"Your quarrel then is with its size and not the fact that Mexico once owned it."

"Best I can recall, the Mexicans took it from the Indians."

"True! But is that not what you Americans did with the rest of your country?"

"It is and I guess they didn't want to show any discrimination so they showed everybody they could take from Mexicans as well."

"You seem to take all such things rather lightly," Madiera de Lopez observed.

"If you want to be serious about it, it wasn't so much

the land that the Texicans wanted as it was their freedom to live upon it. General Santa Ana had other ideas.''

Morgan's eyes met those of Madiera de Lopez and they were locked in a silent exchange of desire. Madiera was beautiful. Her raven hair appeared, at times, almost blue because it was so black. Her eyes, also black, sparkled from the reflected light of crystal glassware. Her nose was slim and her lips thin, moist lines which offered a silent invitation to be kissed.

She wore a black lace *mantilla,* a high-necked, lace-collared black dress, form fitted. The form was full and equally inviting. Morgan could feel the warmth and rigidity between his thighs each time he looked at her. He suspected she sensed as much.

"The meal was excellent," Morgan finally said, pushing back from the table.

"Good! I'm pleased that you enjoyed it." The elder Lopez then silently gestured at his daughter and she stood, nodded in Morgan's direction and left the dining room. Moments later, a big, young Mexican entered the room. He was lavishly dressed and heavily armed. Everyone stood. Morgan was late but he got to his feet.

"Mr. Morgan. Please to make the acquaintance of one of my most trusted *vaqueros.*. This is Dorateo Arango." Neither man spoke but there was a silent contest of hand strength for a few moments. Finally, Arango grinned, withdrew his hand and nodded. Everyone resumed their seats.

The ensuing table talk was of the unimportant again and the newest arrival said nothing. He devoured the meal with considerable relish and then fired up a Cuban cigar. He topped off each hearty puff with a sizeable swallow of brandy. Upon completion of those treats, the young Mexican named Arango proceeded to down two jiggers of Tequila in a toast to his host.

That done, he turned to Morgan and spoke in nearly perfect English. "I hope you will deal with de Lopez. He is a good friend and an honest one. Most important however is the accomplishment itself. You would be serving both the *campensinos* and the *peons*. The peasants and the workers. Think of it well, *señor* Morgan."

Retirement in the de Lopez house came early, at least for the likes of Lee Morgan. Granted, it had been a long and busy day but ten o'clock was often the time when Morgan was getting his second wind. After several attempts at sleep, he opted to give San Antonio the once-over.

Morgan had the distinct feeling that he was being followed but he saw no one and he had not encountered any opposition to his departure. Down on Commerce Street, not too far from the Alamo, Morgan found a saloon. Its name alone prompted his entry.

The *Deguello* was far from plush but it boasted a lively casino and a variety of other forms of entertainment. The name translated to "Ask no quarter and give none"—loosely at least. It was reputed to have been the melody to which the Mexicans made their final storm of the Alamo's walls. In this setting, it brought a smile to Morgan's face.

By midnight, the steely eyed gunman had won himself about seventy-five dollars at the Keno table and decided to quit the place. He cashed in, downed a final drink and stepped into an almost deserted street.

The shot was high! It splintered the wood just inches

above and behind Morgan's head. His gun was in his hand in the flash of gunpowder which accompanied the shot and he fired toward it. He heard a grunt and the thud of a body on a wooden sidewalk.

Instinctively, when the shot had been fired, Morgan went low, drew, rolled and fired. Now, he scrambled for the meager shelter of a darkened doorway. Seconds turned to more than a minute—then two. Stealthily, Morgan eased back onto the street. It was no surprise that not a single soul had exited the saloon to investigate. Unless it was their own personal flight, few men cared to risk their necks for anyone else, much less a total stranger.

Morgan headed across the street in an attempt to find his victim. Someone who, moments before, had been his would-be killer. He was halfway across the street when he heard the voice to his right.

"Coltrane!" Again Morgan dived. This time the shot took off his hat. He fired toward its point of origin but he was certain he'd missed. A shotgun's blast ripped through the night and behind him, a body slammed into a wall. He heard a man running. He got to a crouch, stayed low until he reached his horse and then did a single stirrup ride for more than a block. Finally he pulled himself full into the saddle and rode like hell for the de Lopez spread.

Morgan nearly broke the door to the library down. He stepped inside and found himself facing five drawn guns. He didn't slow down as he walked to the desk and confronted the elder de Lopez who was just getting to his feet.

"I had nothing to do with it, Morgan. I give you my

word. It was my man who fired the shotgun—who saved your life."

"Only two other people outside of this room knew I was coming to San Antonio—and why. You're a damned unconvincing liar, Lopez." Morgan heard the gun hammers click back into position. "I'll kill you before I go down," Morgan continued, "and you know it."

"Yes, Morgan. I do know it so tell me why should I risk dying by even coming in here—by waiting for you? Hmm?" Morgan let reason back into his head. Lopez was right. Or very goddam clever.

"Then *who*, Lopez? If not you, or your men. Who?"

"Sanchez there," Lopez replied, pointing to one of his men, "he was the one with the shotgun. He said he heard a name called out."

"So did I—but it wasn't mine."

"No—it was the name Coltrane. Does that mean anything to you?"

"Not a damned thing," Morgan answered.

"The Double C ranch, Morgan. It is quite near Uvalde. It is large. Very large. Its owner is a woman. Her name is Charity Coltrane."

"Those goddamned bushwhackers didn't mistake me for any woman." Lopez held out a drink. Morgan accepted and down it in one motion. He set the glass on Lopez's desk. "And," he continued almost as though there had been no interruption, "I don't know the Coltranes and never did as far as I can recollect."

"A man of your profession meets many people under many circumstanes. Perhaps you've forgotten."

"Maybe. But not likely."

"There is another possible answer," Lopez said.

"The man you shot tonight did not die immediately. Sanchez came across him when he himself was shifting positions. He too mumbled something which included the name Coltrane and the name Marsh. It somewhat jogged my own memory. As I recall—there was a family dispute a few years ago—before the father of the Double C's present owner died. The feud centered on a son."

"Interesting, Lopez," Morgan said, "but hardly helpful."

"Perhaps this will be." Lopez handed Morgan a thick, leather-bound book. It was a history of Texas cattle ranches. "Look on page thirty-three, Morgan." Morgan considered Lopez, eyed the book and then did as he was bid. A moment later, Morgan's jaw dropped.

"Jeezus!"

"Yes—a remarkable resemblance I'd say. Your features and coloring are those of a man ten years later than that picture. I'd guess you've been mistaken for this Marshall Coltrane, and for someone his reappearance must be very disquieting."

There was no doubt that the man depicted in the book could have easily passed for Lee Morgan—or vice-versa. Side by side perhaps, the differences would be obvious but at a distance—and with several years separating the man in the photograph from his present-day enemies— Morgan made an inviting substitute.

"Seems to me you went to no small amount of trouble to prove to me that you weren't behind tonight, Lopez."

"I did, but with selfish motives. I need your approval. It means the Masters Cartage Company will haul my goods."

"Why them? There are plenty of freight outfits."

"No, Morgan, there are *not*. Those who have not shown fear at my proposal stand to lose too much American business working for me. In the case of the Masters firm they have little to lose. Unless they turn me down."

"And you want freight hauled into Mexico to supply that fancy-dressed *Generalissimo* I met last night. That right?"

"*Si, señor*. That," Lopez grinned, *"Generalissimo,* as you have called him, was born a peasant. His name is —*was* as you were told. Dorateo Arango."

"And now?"

"Francisco Villa. The people—his people have come to call him Pancho."

"He's a revolutionary. The Masters were pretty explicit about staying out of Mexican trouble."

"Pancho Villa *is* a revolutionary, but the *revolucion* is far away. Only now is he beginning to gather support, and if he is to gather enough, he must show that he can equip his army."

"That takes money," Morgan said. Almost sarcastically he added, *"Mucho dinero, señor Lopez."*

"Quite, Mr. Morgan. The *dinero* I can supply. Villa and his men will supply the courage and the skills. Someone must haul much of both—and that will require a little of everything. Do you know of any such party?"

"I'll sleep on it." Morgan stalked out and went to his room. He sensed that he was not alone when he entered. The lamp confirmed his feeling. Madiera Lucia de Lopez was just a wisp away from naked.

"I was beginning to like your father," Morgan said, "until now. I didn't think he'd go this far."

"If my father knew I was here, *señor* Morgan, he would have you tied to a post and shot—tonight!"

"Me?"

"*Si.* He would suspect something more but he would never question me—and he wouldn't believe you."

"And I'm not too inclined to believe you, *señorita.*"

"I am here for one person—for me. My father believes I was raped when I was thirteeen. I wasn't. But that's what he believes. That is why he would not question me. Since then I've known no man. Delgado was but a boy. I am betrothed. It is the way in Mexican aristocracy, *señor* Morgan. I only wish to be a proper wife, but I know nothing of what is expected of me."

"You don't want a man. You want a teacher."

"I want both, *señor* Morgan—and I want you."

Madiera Lopez dropped the negligee and stood in the half light. It played over the supple curves of her dark skin and Morgan could feel the rise of his desire. He resisted in silence but the day's events hurtled through his thoughts. He was, he pondered, an emissary for the Masters Cartage Company of Uvalde, Texas. He was, in the eyes of the elder de Lopez, a lightning fast yankee with questionable courage. Apparently, to others, he was the spitting image of a man with whom someone had a hell of a quarrel—one Marsh Coltrane. If there was a reward for him in all of this, Madiera Lucia de Lopez might be his only chance to collect it. He stripped.

The night air and the moisture from the tip of Morgan's tongue quickly hardened Madiera's nipples. Goose bumps ran up her arms and legs and then melted away as Morgan warmed to his task. At the outset, the Mexican girl's body was limp. Morgan positioned her on the bed to suit his pleasure. In minutes she was transformed from student to participant.

She pressed against him, grinding her hips against his manhood as he manipulated the firmness of her breasts. She moaned softly and Morgan felt a twinge in his gut as his mind relayed a message of caution.

"Quietly," he whispered. She sucked in her breath and nodded. Morgan's body raised and he began an exploratory sojourn toward his ultimate destination. His tongue circled the hardened, dark brown circles which topped her breasts, skittered along her abdomen and lingered for a moment at her navel. Madiera stiffened as he went lower and, at last, he thrust home and found the center of her passion.

After what seemed a very long time, Morgan believed Madiera to be at the very peak of desire. He gently shifted her body to his left, lay down and positioned her atop him. Madiera needed little encouragement— or instruction. She now explored with lips, teeth and tongue. The exchange had brought both the gunman and the woman to the very pinnacle of human desire. They flowed into one, moving together as though they had practiced the event a hundred times before. Blood surged, breath came in short, strained gasps and then their link was welded in a gushing, breathless explosion of flesh against flesh—moisture mingling with moisture.

"Will you ask the Masters to help my father?" The question caught Morgan by surprise. They were the first words spoken by either and they aroused Morgan's original suspicions. Madiera raised to her elbows, turned toward him and kissed him, long but gently on the mouth. "I hope so. It will mean—perhaps once more for us. Maybe twice."

"You're sure as hell worth the risk," Morgan whispered.

"I think," she said, smiling, "that is a *gringo complimento.*"

"*Si, si,*" Morgan said, pulling her close, "it sure as hell is."

Madiera departed. Morgan smoked, had a drink and dropped into the deepest and most restful sleep he'd enjoyed in weeeks.

4

"Hold your goddam horses," Morgan shouted. Ignoring the anger of the plea, Morgan's sunup visitor pounded on the door again. He opened it and came face to face with a scrubby looking gent whose belt seemed over burdened with the task of keeping his girth from spilling down the front of his pants. "Who the hell are you?"

"Sam Tanksley's the name," the man replied and handed Morgan a note.

> We got a special order from a rancher named Jessup down in Cotulla. Wants a wagon load of dynamite brought down from San Antonio. By the time you read this Sam will have the load ready. Shotgun him and then head back to Uvalde.
>
> Lucy Masters

"Shit!" Morgan looked up. "She sent me up here to do a job. I'm not through with it yet."

"You are," Jesus de Lopez said, stepping into view, "if you will tell your boss lady *yes.*" Morgan felt his face flush a little at the sight of Madiera's father. He rubbed his cheeks and eyes to cover whatever might show and then turned away.

"We were supposed to talk this morning," Morgan said, tentatively. He knew the need had been eliminated the night before.

"There is nothing which remains to be said, Mr. Morgan. Is it yes or no?"

"It's yes," Morgan answered, "but with a damned strong condition."

"*Señor?*"

"If you end up being on the wrong side of this little partnership I'll kill you." Morgan's eyes were squinty and he was staring straight into Lopez's face. He gestured behind himself with a sweep of his arms. "And all those *vaqueros* won't stop me. You got that?"

"*Si, señor* Morgan. I have it."

Morgan turned to Sam Tanksley. "You got a load ready?"

"Yep."

"Then give me two minutes and we'll move out." Tanksley nodded and left. Morgan threw his things together and as he started to leave, Jesus de Lopez grabbed his arm.

"I could spare a *vaquero* or two to ride with you."

"Thanks, but we'll be fine. If somebody still wants a piece of me I'd just as soon they'd try again and get it over with. Anyway, you'd best ready yourself for our first job."

"As you wish, *señor*. And God speed, *amigo*." Morgan just nodded.

A hundred miles away, in the luxury of the den of the

SHOTGUN STATION

Double C Ranch, Charity Coltrane had just finished reading a telegraph cable from San Antonio. She winced as she realized the consequences of the failed effort to eliminate the man she believed was Marsh Coltrane. Now, she knew, he was alerted and would be ever watchful of another attempt. The door opened and she saw Kingston.

"Yes, what is it?"

"Mister Railsback is heah," the tall, black man answered in his clipped, West Indian accent. Charity frowned. Jed Railsback was her ramrod. As far as she knew, he had been checking fence lines and line shacks.

"Send him in." Charity poured herself a glass of sherry and then sat down at her desk. Kingston ushered Jed into the room.

"Will there be anything else, Miss Coltrane?"

"No Kingston, not now, thank you." He nodded and took his leave, closing the door behind him.

"You look right off the trail, Jed. What's wrong?"

"Three line shacks burned out and what I figure to be forty to fifty head o' stock missin'. Horse flesh—not beef."

"Damn! It's Marsh. It's that son-of-a-bitch, Marsh!"

"Your brother?" Clearly Jed was shocked.

"He's no kin of mine, Jed—no Coltrane at all."

"Sorry ma'am. I—"

"Never mind." Charity got to her feet and walked around the desk. "You see tracks? I mean signs of riders?" He nodded. "How many?"

"More'n a dozen. Could be eighteen or twenty. Found most o' the tracks in a wallow. Hard to be accurate. They headed north as far as we trailed."

41

"How old?"

"Two or three days."

"North," Charity said to herself. She stared at the floor in thought and then she looked up. "Where is he taking them—toward the mountains?"

"Yes'm. Leastways that's my guess. There may be more gone too—from the west line an' mebbe south."

"There's only one pasture up along the Anacachos big enough to feed and water that much stock."

Jed Railsback nodded. "Rimfire range. Handle two —three hundred head."

"Round up the men. Leave just enough to handle the day work. Have them here in the morning." Charity noted the sudden change of expression of Jed's face. She looked quizzical. His eyes dropped. "Jed?" He shuffled his feet and twisted his hat in his hands. "Damn it, Jed! What the hell is the matter?"

He looked up and took a long, deep breath. "Ma'am. Most of 'em won't ride."

"What the hell do you mean? They won't ride? They work for me, don't they?"

"They're wranglers ma'am—not gunmen."

"They work for the Double C and by God they'll defend the Double C."

"Against a rustler or two—a squatter mebbe—but this here is a gang—paid for killers hired by your— by an outcast Coltrane. It's Coltrane business, ma'am, not the men's."

"Any business that's Double C business is theirs too —or by God they won't have work. Not here," she shouted, thrusting her finger toward the floor, "or on any goddamned ranch in the state of Texas!"

"Ma'am," Jed said, his voice calm and low in tone,

"I'll ride for you—hell—*with* you anywhere. So will a few o' the others—but not most. They won't ride against the likes o' Marsh Coltrane and them what would be sidin' with him."

"Get out!" Charity screamed. Kingston opened the door. Jed was backing toward it and Charity picked up a nearby vase. Her eyes met those of Kingston. She suddenly realized she was not being tough or a Coltrane or a ranch owner. Charity was being a woman. Granted, she was a woman angered—even scorned but this was not the time or the place or the circumstances for such actions. She replaced the vase.

"Get together as many men as you can," she said to Jed. Her voice was firm but soft. Jed smiled. Both men left. Charity sat down behind the big desk. She wanted to bawl. She didn't.

The freight run to Cotulla was uneventful. Pete Jessup and his son, Tom, met the wagon and escorted Morgan and Sam Tanksley to a shed far from the main house. Several men waited to help them unload. One of Jessup's men, inside the darkened building, looked out. His eyes got big and he turned, hurrying still deeper into the shadows. He found a second man.

Jim Kincaid looked up at the sound of Louie Howard's voice.

"Yeah Louie—the wagon here?"

"Jim—he—he's on that wagon." Kincaid looked quizzical. "Marsh Coltrane is ridin' shotgun on that freight wagon." Nearly fifteen years had passed since Marsh Coltrane had gunned down Jim Kincaid's little brother on a muddy street in Del Rio. In Kincaid's memory the act was murder and it was as fresh as this morning's breakfast biscuits.

"Git a shotgun," Kincaid said and pointed upwards. "Git in the loft. No matter what happens to me—blow that son-of-a-bitch all to hell!" Louie Howard nodded, fetched a scattergun, climbed into the loft and disappeared in the darkness. Jim Kincaid got to his feet, drew his revolver, checked it for load and walked toward the light at the end of the warehouse building.

Sam Tanksley's eyes picked up two movements almost simultaneously. The first was the appearance in the doorway of Jim Kincaid, gun drawn. The second was just above him. Sam looked up.

"Morgan—the loft!" The shotgun roared and Sam Tanksley's hat disappeared along with part of the top of his head. Morgan's actions were a blur to the half dozen onlookers. The man in the loft died instantly with a bullet through his chest. Jim Kincaid got off four shots. The first grazed Morgan's left arm. The others were fired as the result of a dying man's reflex actions and went harmlessly into the air.

"Tom—my God—no—no!" The voice was behind Morgan. He dropped and turned, firing at the sound. Tom Jessup stood between Morgan and Pete Jessup. He took Morgan's shot in the forehead.

The entire tragic scenario had unfolded in less than thirty seconds. Two of Jessup's men, his own son and old Sam Tanksley were dead. Lee Morgan didn't know why but he reasoned that there and then was neither the time or place to find out. Several of Jessup's men were making threatening gestures. Only Morgan's gun, still in his hand and still smoking, and their own testimony as to his speed, kept them from making a move. He knew there was courage—false or not—in numbers.

Morgan freed up his horse, leveled his pistol at two of Jessup's men and ordered them to load Sam's body. They complied. Morgan backed up to where he could speak to Pete Jessup.

"I don't know why your men tried to kill me," he said, "but you'd best find out and let the other ones know it was a mistake. You see to it a bank draft gets to the Masters for this load, Mr. Jessup or I'll be back."

Jessup looked up. There were tears in his eyes but Morgan could see no signs of hatred. Jessup nodded. Morgan mounted up and rode out—hard and fast.

Midway back to Uvalde, Morgan realized the possible trouble he could encounter by continuing to haul a dead man. He reined up, found a shallow arroyo and some good sized rocks. He laid Sam Tanksley out and covered him with enough, hopefully, to keep the scavengers away.

"So long, Sam, sorry I didn't get to know you better." Such was Sam Tanksley's funeral.

Uvalde's streets were deserted when Morgan rode in. It was late and it was raining. He was grateful for all the conditions. He turned into the alleyway behind the main street's businesses and worked his way toward the Masters' house. There was a single light burning. It was in the kitchen at the rear of the house. He tethered his mount, stayed to the shadows and finally rapped, lightly on the door. Lucy opened it.

"Mr. Morgan?" She squinted into the darkness in an effort to confirm her utterance. Morgan pushed her aside, entered and then closed the door. "What are you doing back so soon? I didn't expect you until tomorrow. And where's Sam?" She looked back at the door as though expecting her driver to walk through it.

"Is your father here?"

"No—I—," Morgan held up his hand. He went to the front of the house, peering out the front windows. The street was empty. The rain was falling harder. He returned to the kitchen.

"Fix a pot of coffee. It's going to be a long night."

"Damn you! What is going on?"

"Fix the coffee. When your father gets here you'll find out as much as I know. I don't intend to repeat the story anymore often than I have to, but I will tell you this much. You've got a deal with de Lopez."

"Good—I—I was beginning to wonder if there had been trouble."

"There was. Sam Tanksley is dead." Lucy's jaw dropped. "Like I said—when your dad gets here—you'll hear the rest." Morgan pointed for her to resume making the coffee. She nodded. He could see the moisture in her eyes.

Morgan had sipped coffee, smoked and made several trips back and forth to the front of the house to peer outside. He had said nothing. Nearly forty-five minutes had elapsed since his arrival. Lucy was growing increasingly impatient—even a bit angry.

"When's your dad due back?"

"Anytime now," Lucy replied, "but I told you once before, Morgan, I'm a full partner. We've been hit again, lost another driver and you obviously think someone is on your trail. I want to know right now just what the hell happened."

"To be honest about it," Morgan answered, "I was hoping you and your dad might be able to tell me. I mean not *what* happened but *why*." Both of them heard the buggy. Lucy peered through the kitchen window.

She turned back to Morgan, smiling.

"Dad's back."

"Good."

"More coffee?"

"Yeah."

"How about something to eat? Pie maybe? It's apple. I have some cookies too."

"Pie's fine," Morgan said. The back door opened and Luke Masters stepped inside. He too showed surprise at Morgan's presence but it was obvious to Lucy that he had something far more pressing on his mind that the unexpected return of one of his hired hands.

"Coffee, Dad?"

"Whiskey," he replied. "A glass full." He shed his slicker and hat. He took the whiskey, downed about half of it and then, almost ignoring Morgan's presence, he spoke to Lucy. "The last of our business is gone," he said. "Two contracts with the Del Rio Merchants' Association and the lumber deal in San Angelo."

"Dad—*why?* What happened?"

"It's what's *been* happening. I told them we had a new shotgun rider. Better protection. God," he continued, his eyes shifting from his daughter to Morgan and then down at the floor. "I even lied to them."

"About what?" Morgan asked.

"The lumber deal. I told them it was way bigger than it is—uh—*was.* I even gave the name of a banker friend of mine for verification." Luke Masters sat down now, almost as though he'd been struck a blow. "They already had a telegraph cable from Del Rio. They caught me in my own lie. He looked up. "They tore our contracts up right there in front of God and everybody and the Merchant's Association president called me a liar right to my face."

Lucy went to her father, kneeling in front of him. He turned his face away but she reached up and forced him to look at her. "It's all right, Dad. Believe me. It's all right. I understand. And we're not licked. Not yet." He frowned. Lucy turned. "Tell him, Morgan." Luke Masters looked toward the gunman.

"You've got a deal with de Lopez."

Luke grinned sardonically. "It was probably the rumors about that deal that finished us with the others. Damn! I hope it pays well."

"It will," Morgan said, "if we survive to do it."

"What do you mean?"

"Sam Tanksley and I delivered that load of dynamite down to Pete Jessup. Two of Jessup's men cut loose on me—along with Jessup's son. Sam's dead. I buried him along the trail back."

"Good God a-mighty. Why—I've known Pete Jessup for years. Long before I came to Uvalde. I don't understand it."

"It wasn't Pete," Morgan said. "Matter of fact—he tried to stop his son."

"And you—you had to—" Morgan nodded. "There's another son." Morgan saw Lucy's eyes grow large and her mouth opened as though the was about to speak. She looked at Morgan but no words came out.

"Another son?"

"Hobie. He had five years in Yuma for robbery and a shootin' I think. He's out now. Last I heard, he was in Mexico. He won't take well to this, Morgan, an' he's not likely to listen to his daddy."

"First things first," Morgan said. "I got shot at by Jessup's men—and up in San Antonio. If it hadn't been for one of Lopez's *vaqueros*, I might not have made it to Jessup's place."

"You got somethin' behind you that we don't know about?" Luke asked, pushing Lucy away and getting to his feet. Morgan could sense Masters' sudden aggression.

"Probably lots of things," Morgan said, coolly, "but none of them would have involved a couple of saddle tramps like the ones that jumped me in San Antonio."

"An' Jessup's hands?"

"Never saw 'em before—or heard tell of 'em either. That's the fact of it, Mr. Masters."

"Then *why*, Morgan?"

"Ever hear the name Coltrane?" Lucy and her father looked at each other, incredulous. Then they both stared at Morgan. "Well?"

"Of course. The Coltrane ranch is one of the biggest in Texas. The Double C." Luke Masters gestured to the southwest by poking his thumb over his right shoulder. "The house is about twelve miles from here."

Lucy suddenly stepped toward Morgan and he could see flashes of anger in her eyes as she spoke. "You saying Coltrane men jumped you?"

"No—the men who jumped me both *called* me that name."

"What?"

"They hollered it out at me just before they made their plays."

"But there are no Coltrane men. That spread is owned by Charity Coltrane—left to her lock, stock and barrel by her daddy."

"Well, Miss Masters," Morgan said, half grinning, "I don't think any of those bushwhackers mistook me for any woman ranch owner." Both Morgan and Lucy now looked to the elder Masters. He was looking toward the window, obviously deep in thought.

"I was just speaking to Charity Coltrane," Lucy continued, speaking to Morgan but still looking at her father. "She and I had, let me say, a minor disagreement awhile back. I was hoping we could bury the hatchet and do some business."

"You mentioned this woman's daddy."

"He's dead—quite a good long time now—before dad and I ever came to Uvalde."

"A brother," Luke Masters suddenly blurted out, whirling. "I remember readin' about a big family feud. I've heard tales since we been here too."

"Yes," Lucy agreed, tentatively, "I—I heard some talk."

"Best I can recollect," Luke continued, "this—brother—or whatever—well, he was an illegitimate son of the old man's. Anyways—there was a fallin' out an' the old man run 'im off."

"And when was all this?" Morgan asked.

"Got to be near a dozen years ago. We been in Uvalde for ten. Charity Coltrane owned the Double C when we got here—and still does. Runs the place by herself—hard and tough." Luke Masters looked now at his daughter. "We'll get no business out o' the Double C."

"Don't be too sure, Daddy. She didn't shoot me on the spot."

"She given to that kind of thing?" Morgan asked.

"She is," Luke replied. "Totes a pair of Colts on her hips that she's run more than one cowhand off with."

"And you're sayin' you think I'm being taken for this bastard brother?" Luke nodded. "Well—it ties in with what de Lopez told me."

Morgan went on to explain what he'd heard from the Mexican in San Antonio and, finally, about the photograph he'd seen. "I'll have to admit there was a helluva ·likeness. If time has treated Marsh Coltrane about the same as it's treated me—well—we could pass for kin."

"If my memory serves me at all, Morgan, any of the Double C hands that spot you will be out to gun you. Charity would kill you on sight."

"I don't take kindly to being a walking target," Morgan said. "I'd just as soon face Miss Coltrane down and show her the mistake before one of her gun hawks gets lucky."

"There's only one reasonable way to handle this," Lucy said. "I've only just spoken to Charity so I'll ride out there and invite her to come to dinner tomorrow. It'll be a switch from what we talked about—you going out there, Daddy. I don't think she'll refuse. It's certainly better to have her face Morgan here than try to get him on Double C land."

"He'd never get by that fancy, marble entryway."

"Whatever is done—and where—best get done quick. Lopez will want us soon—and when word gets back to the Double C about San Antonio, Miss Charity Coltrane may not feel so charitable."

Morgan's allusion to Charity's name brought a snicker from Lucy even under the circumstances. The evening had been one of mixed blessings and tension was high. It was Luke Masters who suggested a final drink and then a good night's sleep. No one argued against either elixir.

5

Jed Railsback had pulled together about twenty men from the Double C's contingent. He did his best to discourage Charity from riding with them. It was a futile effort. They worked north and west for three days, checking stock, riding into half a dozen box canyons and finally converging on the rolling meadow known as the Rimfire range. It was obvious there had been both cattle and horse stock there. But not for more than a week. Discouraged and seething inside, Charity ordered the search ended and the riders started back for the Double C.

"Miss Charity," Jed said, pointing to the east, "I'd guess that smoke to be the Larkin place." Charity reined up. She eyed the horizon, took her bearings and then nodded. "I could take a couple o' men and have a look-see."

"We'll all ride in. If there's trouble, at least there's enough of us to make a difference." Jed agreed and turned the men toward the ridge. They had covered less than half the distance to its crest when several shots rang out off to their left. Again, Charity called a halt. This time, they could see someone—a lone rider. The rider stood in the stirrups and was waving an upraised rifle back and forth.

"Ride down there and find out who that is and what they want," Charity ordered. Jed Railsback nodded and took the job on himself. Charity watched as Jed neared his destination. Another shot. The lone rider fell from the saddle. Two more shots and Charity saw Jed go down—but she was not certain if he'd been hit or was simply trying to save himself. A moment later, half a dozen riders appeared from the trees just beyond where the single rider had signalled. They began firing toward the Double C riders. Charity yelled for them to head for the ridge. It was exactly what they wanted.

Jed pulled himself into a firing position and began pumping shots from a Henry toward the half dozen riders. His marksmanship proved worthwhile and he forced their withdrawal. Too late, Jed turned to warn Charity of the frontal assault he knew would charge over the ridge. Indeed, it came.

If the Double C's hands were nothing else, they were not short on courage. Faced with twice their own numbers, they displayed amazing marksmanship and a collective tenacity which no doubt was a major contributing factor to such low casualties. Nonetheless, the Double C lost six good men that night and Charity Coltrane lost her favorite mount. Jed, in a dashing display of heroics, rode into heavy fire and pulled Charity from beneath her mortally wounded horse. Jed took a bullet in the back of his left leg as they galloped away.

Two reports awaited Charity Coltrane the following

morning. She had risen before sunup, dressed in the buckskins which she normally wore only at roundup time, strapped on her twin Colts and breakfasted, with Jed, in the Double C's huge library. It was Jed Railsback, his leg tender but not debilitating, who made the first report.

"The Larkins were burned out and run off and their ramrod was killed."

"The riders who hit us?"

"The same."

"Identification?"

"None at the Larkin place—but—" Jed halted, cleared his throat and started to speak again. Charity didn't wait.

"It's Marsh, isn't it?"

"Yes'm—but, well, it's worse'n we figgered."

"What do you mean?"

"He killed two hands down on the Jessup spread at Cotulla." Jed took a deep breath, held it a moment and then released it with the words, "An' Jessup's boy— Tom."

"Dear God. I know Marsh hates me—but *this*. Why others? They have nothing to do with Daddy . . . or the Double C."

"They would, Miss Charity, if'n Marsh Coltrane owned the Double C."

Charity stiffened and her eyes grew dark and her countenance sinister. "He'll kill every man-jack on this spread, all the stock and then me before that happens, Jed."

"Yes'm—I know that—an' I think he'd do it in the blink of an eye too. He's even turnin' them in town ag'in you." Charity considered the statement. She was not the most sociable ranch owner in Texas—at least with those in the town of Uvalde—but aside from a skirmish or two over something none too important, she'd never really made any dark enemies. "The sheriff's here, ma'am."

Lund Taylor removed his hat, nodded at Jed and then said, "Ma'am, I come to apologize to you and tell you that I'm callin' in deputies from Del Rio an' informin' the U.S. Marshal up in Abilene. We'll see to it that Marsh Coltrane gets his due."

"Where is he, Sheriff? You know, don't you?"

Sheriff Lund had shared a rumor he'd picked up in town with Jed. He frowned at Jed now, for it had not been his intention to share it with Charity.

"I work for the lady, Lund, an' I happen to know she was plannin' some business with them folks in a few days." Now Charity was doubly puzzled.

"I heard he's workin' with the Masters over to the freight line. He was ridin' shotgun with Sam Tanksley when the francas happened down to the Jessup place."

Charity's face paled. She had spoken to Lucy Masters only a few days ago. They had, more or less, agreed to bury the hatchet. It appeared now that Lucy's intent was to bury it to the hilt—in Charity Coltrane's back. Charity got to her feet.

"Jed. Get a horse saddled for me."

"Ma'am, I can't let you—" It was as far as Lund Taylor got. Charity had one Colt drawn and leveled at the big sheriff's belly. "You can't go keepin' your own law anymore'n anybody else."

"As of right now, Sheriff, the law has nothing to do with this. As of right now—it's Double C business— family, more or less. Don't decide that I wouldn't use this, Lund. Believe me—I will.''

"I don't think you will, ma'am," Lund said. He started toward her and Jed, already starting out the door, turned, drew his pistol and brought its barrel down on the back of the sheriff's head. Lund Taylor crumpled into a heap.

"You doubt me too, Jed?"

Jed Railsback looked straight into Charity Coltrane's eyes and shook his head. "No *ma'am*—I sure didn't. That's how's come I did what I did. No need to start the shootin' any sooner'n we have to." Jed knelt and checked the sheriff's breathing and the knot on the back of his head. That done, he stood up. "He'll be hurtin' an' madder'n hell—but he'll live. I'll fetch a horse for you, Miss Charity."

As Charity prepared to ride into Uvalde and face down her family's black sheep, Lee Morgan had made a decision of his own. Several people were dead purely because he looked like someone he wasn't. Morgan was never much to ally himself with lawmen but this situation dictated unusual action. He was dressed and ready to slip out of the house when Lucy confronted him.

"You crazy, Morgan, or plannin' just to ride out and disappear?"

"I look pretty bad in either of those descriptions. But so far this has been my trouble and not yours, Granted, you've lost some business, but you've got Lopez now. If this thing is handled right, the Coltrane woman will learn the truth and nobody else needs to die."

"If you ride to the Double C you'll die."

"Didn't plan on it," Morgan replied. "That would be

the crazy part you asked me about.''

Lucy eyed him. She suddenly had a twinge inside. It surprised her. She couldn't help but wonder if Morgan had somehow detected it. She identified it as *desire*. Lee Morgan was a man she *desired*. She shook off the feeling and said, ''Then you're high-tailin' it?''

''That would be the other part—disappearing. Nope —neither one. Uvalde's got law. The sheriff can bring Miss Coltrane into town. We can meet. He can get verification of who I am.''

''Real easy, eh? Just walk out and go see the sheriff.''

Morgan looked puzzled. That was exactly what he'd planned.

''You look outside this morning?'' Lucy tipped her head to the right toward the window. Morgan moved over to it, pulled the curtain aside and peered out. Five men stood just beyond the picket fence which ran along the front of the Masters' house. ''There's at least two more—mebbe three—out back.''

''Shit!'' Morgan moved into the kitchen and got his rifle.

''What's that for?''

''That should be obvious.''

''It isn't. We can't stand 'em off—not in here. You go out and you might get ten feet.''

''Well then—Miss Masters—you got a plan?''

''None that really excites me. Two of those men out front work—or *did* work for Pete Jessup. I really don't think they'll give an ear to much palaver. I'm hoping they'll believe my promise to deliver you to them.''

''And just when do you plan to make that promise?''

''Already have, Mr. Morgan. I got this reply.'' She handed him a note.

It's all up to Hobie. He'll be here by ten this
morning.

Morgan read, frowned and looked up. "Hobie?"

"The other Jessup boy. Remember?" Morgan
nodded. "Well, it's pretty obvious that he's not in
Mexico anymore."

"Yeah." Morgan peered out again and then asked
"Where's your dad?"

"Still sleeping."

"He know about this?"

"Not yet."

"If I'm figuring right—and the same way you are—
those boys aren't going to let anybody out of this house
until Hobie Jessup arrives."

"You're figuring right, Morgan—the same as me.
Dad too—when he finds out."

"Send them another note—or whatever you did
before. Tell them I'm not Coltrane. Tell them I can
prove I'm not."

"Morgan—Tom Jessup is dead. If what I've heard
about Hobie Jessup is true, it wouldn't make a damn if
you were Jesus himself. Hobie will kill you—or try—
whoever the hell you are."

"*Hobie?* Hobie Jessup?" Lucy's father came down
the stairs. Morgan stayed by the window while Lucy
poured the elder Masters some coffee and brought him
up to date on the turn of events. Luke Masters listened,
sipped his coffee and then got up and went back
upstairs. He reappeared a few minutes later fully
dressed and armed with a long barreled shotgun.

"Dad—put that damned thing down." Luke ignored

his daughter and started toward the door. "Dad!" Morgan turned. Luke Masters was reaching for the doorknob.

"Hold it, Mr. Masters," Morgan shouted, "there's a rider coming down the street. Could be Hobie Jessup." Luke turned the knob but he held back from opening the door. Lucy had hurried to the window and Morgan pulled back the curtain still further so that she might get a look. "Would you know Jessup on sight?"

"I doubt it. I saw his picture once or twice but that was—I don't know—several years ago." Lucy had looked at Morgan as she answered, now she turned back to look out. Her mouth opened. "My God—that's Charity Coltrane." Luke Masters now joined Lucy and Morgan at the window. Charity was still a third of a block away and two of the men had stepped into her path.

"Looks like they're squabblin'," Luke said.

"Yeah," Morgan said, laconically, "which of 'em gets to kill me."

"You think Charity Coltrane knows you're here?"

"Don't know—just seems strange—her showin' up right now."

"By God—this ain't right," Luke Masters said. "I'm a prisoner in my own home—me and mine. I'll not tolerate it a minute longer." Morgan stepped between Luke and the door. "This is *my* house, Mr. Morgan, and I'll thank you to respect them what live there and their wishes."

"I not only respect you," Morgan said, "I've come to like you. That's why I can't let you go out there—not just yet."

"Morgan! Dad! My God—they're shooting!" A shot

smashed into the window about a foot above Lucy's head. Morgan shoved both Lucy and her dad to the floor and then crouched by the window. By then, shots were being fired in both directions. Morgan saw two of Jessup's men drop. One man he guessed was a Coltrane rider got hit.

"Double C ranch men riding with Miss Coltrane."

"Morgan," Lucy screamed, "there's an attic—an access to the roof from there. Maybe you can—" Morgan didn't need any more coaching. He took two stairs at a time. While he wasn't at all certain that Hobie Jessup wouldn't shoot first and ask questions later, the Coltrane hands had run off Jessup's men—front and back. Morgan *did* feel comfortable that Charity Coltrane would at least *ask* if the man she wanted was there before she vented her anger on the Masters. By then—if his plan held—he'd be mounted up and could draw them off the house.

By the time Morgan reached the roof, Charity Coltrane was at the front door. He heard her clearly. "Open up, Lucy, or my men will do it for you. I'm here to get Marshall Coltrane."

Morgan moved to the backside of the house and looked down. There were only two men moving about. He reckoned they were Double C hands still looking for any of the Jessup bunch. He eased down to a porch roof, edged forward until he could drop the remaining six feet, waited until the men had their backs to him and then dropped. They both turned. He'd already pulled his gun.

"Don't do it," he warned them. "I don't want to have to kill you just to prove you're wrong. But I will." One of them got his hand on the butt of his gun.

Morgan cocked his. The man's hand moved away and his arm went limp.

"You're a dead man, Coltrane, no matter what happens now."

"I'm not Coltrane, but right now, that doesn't seem to matter much. Turn around, drop the rigs, carefully and quietly. Then lie down. Face down." The men complied. By the time they had, Morgan had slipped around the corner of a woodshed and headed for the hotel casino and bar. If he was to make a stand, win, lose, or draw, that was the place to do it.

Behind him, Lucy Masters had opened the door for Charity.

"Move back," Charity ordered. She punctuated the command with a movement of the barrel of one of her Colts. Lucy backed inside. Charity saw Luke. "Put down the shotgun."

"You're wrong, Miss Coltrane. The man workin' for us is *not* Marshall Coltrane."

Charity ignored Luke Masters' statement, waited until he had complied with her command and then ordered both him and Lucy to sit.

"Jed, get in here and search the house. Bring a couple of the men with you." The back door opened. Lucy tensed. Charity moved over to her, pushed her back in the chair and leveled her pistol at the archway which led into the kitchen. Jed Railsback and two men came through the front door. One of the Coltrane men who'd been out back now entered the room.

"He's not here, Miss Charity. He came off the roof. Caught me'n Billy flat footed but he didn't git no horse. He's on foot." Charity's eyes flashed as she glanced down at Lucy. Charity holstered her gun and then back-handed Lucy, hard, across the cheek. Lucy winced and jerked back. Charity slapped her again, this time cutting her lip. Luke started to get up but the man from the back shoved him back into the chair.

"Where's Billy?"

"Tryin' to follow Marsh," came the reply. "Looked like he might have headed into town."

"Jed—take all the men you need. Get him. But I want him livin' if it's at all possible."

"Hank—you stay here and keep an eye on these two. If they so much as breath wrong—kill 'em!"

"Damn you, Charity Coltrane. You're wrong! He's not Marshall. His name is Morgan. Lee Morgan." Charity struck again. Lucy fell back into the chair, tears stinging her eyes.

There was no rear entrance to the lower level of the hotel. Morgan went to the far end of the building, eased along it until he reached the front and then checked the street in both directions.

Satisfied that he could reach the entrance unseen, Morgan made his move. Halfway there, he heard a horse, galloping hard, behind him. He stopped and turned.

"Coltrane. Marshall Coltrane. You're under arrest.' Sheriff Lund Taylor pulled up short, dropped from the saddle, freeing his Winchester in the same motion. He levered a shell into the chamber. Just then, two more men, riding hell bent for leather, rounded the corner behind the sheriff. Both had pistols drawn.

"Sheriff—behind you," Morgan yelled. Lund Taylor heard the horses but his reflex action was directed at Lee Morgan. He fired. He probably heard the two shots which were fired almost at the same time behind him. It was less likely that he felt them, although both hit home. Lund Taylor was dead before he hit the ground.

Taylor's shot at Morgan had been just a fraction of an inch too high. It took Morgan's hat off but the agile gunman had dropped to one knee, drawing at the same time. His skills, both inherent and practiced, once again paid dividends. Both riders tumbled from their saddles. Morgan got to his feet, stayed low and half dived into the hotel just below the bat wing doors.

"Everybody stand fast," he shouted. He looked around quickly, taking stock of potential trouble. About half a dozen men were inside—plus the barkeep and the man at the desk. None of them moved.

Nearly two blocks away, Charity Coltrane, Lucy and Luke Masters and Charity's men had all heard the shots. All of them moved from the house quickly and ran toward the sound of the gunfire.

"It's Hobie Jessup," a voice yelled as Charity and her men ran by. Billy Hall was emerging from between two buildings. The group halted. Billy ran to them, somewhat out of breath. "I think Marsh is in the hotel. I didn't see too much but he gunned down the sheriff and two of Jessup's men. There are a dozen or more of them at the far end of town."

"Lund Taylor's dead?" The question came from Lucy. Billy nodded. "You sure, Morgan? The man in the hotel did it?"

"Well—I—I can't say fer sure. I saw him fire. It coulda been Jessup's men. Ever'thing happened mighty fast."

Charity Coltrane turned to look for the rest of her men. They too had now moved up the street. About fifteen of them. She shouted orders to Jed Railsback.

"Take seven or eight of the men and move down Center Street. I'll take the rest and move straight ahead. We'll flush Marsh out. Try to talk to Jessup, but if he won't listen, do what you have to." Jed frowned. Luke Masters now walked up.

"You're turnin' a mistake into an all out war, Mizz Coltrane. I'm givin' you my solemn oath. That man in the hotel is not your brother. What I seen an' heard—even from him—well, he sure enough looks like Marsh Coltrane. But he's *not*." Now, for the first time, Charity looked straight into Luke Masters' eyes. She had listened. She'd heard! She was questioning silently. Wondering.

"Miss Coltrane, I want this thing settled as much as you," Jed Railsback said, "but I got to side with Masters here. We're gettin' into a war we don't need. We oughta be sure first, *dead* sure."

"If you're lying to me," Charity said, looking first at Luke—then at Lucy, "I swear on my father's grave I'll hunt you down and kill you." She turned to Jed. "Stay put."

"Ma'am?"

"I'm going into that hotel. I'm going to find out one way or another."

"Mizz Charity, I—"

"You *what*, Masters? You lied?"

"No!"

"Then this—this man Morgan shouldn't have any reason to gun me down, should he?"

"No," came the reply, weakly.

"Miss Charity," Jed said, anxiously, "there's still Jessup."

"You and the men keep an eye on them. Warn them

off if you can, but I don't want anybody else shot who doesn't have to be.''

"Please, Miss Charity, I—''

"You'll do as you're told, Jed—like always—if you're still working for me." Jed knew Charity Coltrane's mind if he didn't know much else. He knew that once it was set, there was no changing it. He nodded.

Charity kept close to the building as she walked the distance to the hotel. She reached the door without incident. She paused long enough to scan the street still ahead of her. She could see no movement, no signs of life. Her eyes trailed back along the rooftops and then down to the street. She winced when she saw the bodies of Jessup's men and that of Lund Taylor. They had often quarreled but deep within each had been a silent respect for the other. Charity looked in both directions one last time and then pushed her way into the hotel.

"I'll guess you to be Charity Coltrane of the Double C ranch." All the patrons were gathered in one corner of the room. The barkeep stood at the near end of the bar, both hands in plain sight. Midway along the bar, back toward the direction from which Charity had come, stood Lee Morgan.

"I'll be damned!" Charity stepped closer. "You're a shade too tall but outside of that I'd gun you in a minute.''

"Lee Morgan. Until now I never gave a damn about bein' bigger than my dad. Taller anyway. Right now, I'm grateful for that extra two inches.''

"You're a ringer for Marsh Coltrane—outside of the height. I owe you—and some other folks—an apology.''

Morgan eyed the twin Colts. "You keeping those holstered is all the apology I need. I've never killed a woman. Hate to start now."

Charity smirked. "You've even got Marsh's ego. What the hell makes you so certain you *could* kill me?"

"Only that I'd take less chances with you than I would with a man—just because I'm *not* so certain."

"How about San Antonio? And the incident down on the Jessup spread? You?"

"Me."

"I guess I can't fault you for trying to stay alive."

Morgan offered up a half smile. "I appreciate that, Miss Coltrane."

"It's not over you know. Hobie Jessup isn't near as good a listener as I am, and he lost kin."

"From what I've heard, Hobie Jessup runs a mean streak—kin or no kin."

"I'll try to talk to him."

"Thanks, but I'll do my own talking. It's not your fight now."

"Maybe—maybe not. Depends on which of you killed the sheriff."

"Yeah. I was wondering when you'd get around to that question."

"What's your answer, Mr. Morgan?"

"Two two gunnies out there on the street were responsible."

"And you took them out?"

"I did. No reason except I was their ultimate target. The sheriff just happened to get in the way. He wasn't a very good listener either."

"Oh shit!" The barkeep shouted the words and then dived for the shelter of the mahogany bar. The words shifted Morgan's attention, just for a split second, to the speaker. The barkeep's eyes were upraised—the balcony above and behind Morgan.

Morgan's right hand produced his pistol even as he dived, twisting to his left and falling backwards. The last thing he saw before he was completely turned around was the blue-gray smoke belching from the barrels of Charity Coltrane's twin forty-fives. Morgan's own shots, two of them, were in proximity to Charity's and all four homed in on the two men on the balcony. One of them managed a shot of his own but it was high and harmless. Both fell forward, through the balustrade, and crashed into the tables below.

Morgan, his experience dictating continued movement until he had completely weighed the results of the confrontation, rolled clear over and came back to his feet. The bat wing doors opened and a man stepped through, drew and fired at Charity. The bullet took her down, ripping through the fleshy part of her upper left shoulder. Morgan killed the man with a single shot. He tumbled backwards and landed outside.

"Okay, Coltrane—unless you want an all out war— you face me." Morgan was already kneeling by the wounded girl.

"I'm—I'm fine. Damn!" Charity looked up. There were tears in her eyes. "It hurts. I've never been shot before."

"It hurts. Good incentive to keep from getting shot again," Morgan said, "and you're right. You're fine. Bullet went clean through."

"Coltrane!" It was the voice from outside again. "You got thirty seconds, then we start a street war."

"That would be Hobie Jessup," Charity said. "He's

good. Damned good—so I've heard."

Lee Morgan stood up and began reloading. "I'm not Marshall Coltrane, Jessup. My name is Lee Morgan. I'm sorry about your brother but he tried to kill me. I don't want to be responsible for taking two sons away from the same father. So ride out. Leave it be, Jessup."

"You got fifteen seconds left mister an' I don't give a tinker's damn *who* you are."

"Yeah," Morgan said to himself, "I figured you wouldn't."

"Watch him, Morgan," Charity warned, getting to her feet. She staggered a little but waved off Morgan's attempt to help her. "I've got some good men out there. I think they'll keep Jessup's hands busy. If you take him out it'll be over."

"I'll take him out," Morgan said.

Hobie Jessup wore a double rig, butts forward, no tie downs. Morgan had seen the style before. A practiced hand with such a rig could be among the best. Morgan figured Jessup to be practiced. He stepped through the bat wings, stopped, shifted his weight just slightly to his left leg and let his right arm hang loose. Both of Jessup's hands were poised in front of him, ready for the cross-draw move. Inside of five seconds, the two gunmen had sized each other up. Rigs, styles, weapons, general demeanor. Unlike the gentlemanly duels of mid-century, these men were merely practicing their trade. No delayed moments of honor—just sizing up the competition.

Morgan's peripheral vision had given him a summary of the situation. Both the Double C hands and Jessup's had moved to within twenty-five feet of one another. Just across the street and less than a third of a block away were Lucy and Luke Masters. Outside of seeing those things in general and eyeing Jessup's armament when he exited the hotel, Morgan's eyes were affixed to Hobie Jessup's. There would be no more talk. The odor of the shootout inside was still fresh in Morgan's nostrils. The roar of the heavy caliber weapons in the confines of so small a space still rattled around in his head. Such a sound always brought back the memory of the day Buckskin Frank Leslie faced down Kid Curry.

That shootout had been in the cookhouse at the Spade Bit Ranch. Frank Leslie died that day, but he'd outlived Kid Curry! Lee Morgan had since outlived a lot of men who'd tried him. Everyone of them had, or so they believed, a good reason for trying him. Now, Hobie Jessup had a good reason. And he tried.

Hobie cleared leather with both weapons. He aimed and fired both—as Morgan reckoned—a practiced hand. Even as he squeezed off a shot from each, however, he was firing into a fatal blast from a short barreled Smith & Wesson. The bullets from Hobie Jessup's guns went high and buried themselves in the rotting facade of the Hotel *La Cucaracha*. Hobie blinked, his jaw dropped. He glanced down at his chest. Morgan didn't know if he was still alive then or not. A moment later, he fell in the street, face down. Morgan knew then. Hobie Jessup was dead!

6

Charity woke up screaming. She winced as a sharp pain burned through the wound in her shoulder. She heard her Mexican housemaid hurrying along the hall outside the bedroom. She felt like a fool. No. More like a little girl. The pampered daughter of a well-do-do Texas cattleman and very much afraid of the things, unseen but always heard, which only seem to manifest themselves in the dark.

"*Señorita* Charity," the maid said, rapping lightly on the door. "Are you all right?"

"Yes, Maria, fine, thank you. I had a bad dream, that's all."

"Can I get you anything?" Charity started to say no but she felt wide awake and still shaky.

"Some hot cocoa, Maria, please."

"*Si señorita*. I'll bring it right up."

"Never mind. I'll be down in a few minutes." Charity threw some cold water on her face, dried it and looked in the mirror. Her eyes were red and puffy. Her shoulder hurt and she still had a lump in her throat from witnessing the scene at the Double C after she had returned three days earlier.

Four of her best ranch hands were dead. Among them Lige Brewster. While she and Jed and most of the best men were in town, on what proved to be a witch hunt, the real culprits had struck home. Stock had been butchered or run off, several out buildings burned and anyone who attempted a defense—murdered. They included, besides Lige, the Chinese cook, Li Sung, a Mexican stable hand named Sancho who was almost like a son to Maria and a Negro stable boy named Joad. Most had been shot down. Charity's nightmares, however, centered on the death of Li Sung. He was found hanging from a ceiling beam in the den. His throat had been cut.

Jed Railsback had wanted to gather every man available and move out at once to find the perpetrators —raiders who had hit more than a score of ranches in the area during the past three months. Charity was adamant. No. She feared a return of the gang to the Double C and she did not intend that it be left undefended again. Instead, she set the men to the task of cleaning up, repairing and—the most gruesome task —burial of the dead.

Charity sat alone now, sipping her cocoa. She ordered Maria back to bed. It was just past four in the morning, one of her favorite times of the day. The false dawn was near. It roused the birds and she could hear them chirping merrily. She loved the isolation. She loved the frontier life. Mostly, she loved the Double C ranch. At that moment, she was fearful for its life.

Charity finished he cocoa and returned to her room. She entertained, ever so briefly, the idea of going back to bed. She knew it would prove useless to try to sleep.

She returned to the kitchen, heated some water and went back to her room to wash up. She stood nude—eyeing herself in the mirror. Her body was lithe, curvaceous. Desirable, she thought.

The cold air hardened her nipples and, without understanding, she felt an impulse to touch them. She did. It felt good. She tweaked them gently. She sucked in her breath. She let her hands slide along her rib cage, down along her waist and then on to her thighs. "My God," she thought, "what have I come to—doing this?" Still, she couldn't stop. How long had it been since she had been with a man—any man—for any reason save business? She couldn't remember. She closed her eyes and let her fingers touch and explore. Suddenly, in her mind's eye, she saw the face, then the form of Lee Morgan. She jerked herself back to reality. She was blushing. She didn't finish washing. She just got dressed.

Several of the townspeople had approached Luke Masters in the day or so following the biggest event in Uvalde's history. They wanted Luke to entice Lee Morgan into putting on the sheriff's badge. At least, so they said, until they could find someone permanent. Morgan and badges didn't mix. Luke tried, Morgan won out. On the third day, the morning of Charity's early awakening, Luke was scheduled to visit the Double C and talk about a freight contract. Lucy was scheduled to meet with Pete Jessup. He knew what had happened but Pete was the Jessup with brains. His two boys had always walked on trouble's edge. Now both had fallen into its chasm.

While the Masters were so engaged, Morgan, along

with Cimmaron Dakis—old Alkali, the last teamster still working for the line—had a run to make to Eagle Pass. It was southwest of Uvalde about sixty miles distant. Alkali called the run the last real heat a man had to suffer just before he went to hell.

About midway along the run, one during which neither man had spoken a word to the other, Cimmaron Dakis issued a challenge.

"Morgan, saw your shootin' t'other day. Purty good."

"Thanks."

"Saw a blacksnake draped over your saddle." Alkali turned now and looked, smiling, into Morgan's face. "Kin you use that too?"

"I've been known to."

"Good as you use that iron you tote?"

"Probably not. But good enough."

"Good 'nuff to earn yourself a quart o' sippin' liquor down to *señora* Gordo's place in the Pass?"

Morgan smiled. "*Señora* Gordo? Unless I've forgotten all my Mex *gordo* means—"

"Yep—just that—*fat*. Last I seed her she come close to weighin' in at three hunnert." Alkali guffawed. "Hot as it gits in this Godforsaken hole it could freeze a man up come nighttime. Now me—I kin enjoy a woman like the *señora*. Got some meat on her bones. Not like Miss Lucy or that there Coltrane gal. No, sir. *Señora* Gordo'll keep ya from freezin' to death."

"Or much of anything else from the sounds of it." Alkali guffawed.

"Yes sir, that'd be just about right."

"So what are you proposing, Alkali? I mean—with the blacksnake."

"Got a stretch o' trail up ahead what the skinners call Rattler Run. Snakes layin' on top o' the·rocks on both sides o' the trail. Man what snaps off the most heads in two miles wins hisself a quart.".

"And how will I know when we've gone two miles?" Morgan was half joking when he made the inquiry but Alkali's response told the gunman much about the tough old teamster.

"Why I'll tell you when, sonny. Made this run a hunnert times or more. It's 'xactly two miles between a big ol', half rotted stove pipe cactus an' a half dome boulder what sits on your side o' the trail."

Morgan grinned. "You've covered, Alkali." He crawled to the back of the wagon, stretched a bit to reach his horse and crawled back up front with his blacksnake whip. He hadn't used it for quite a spell and he had the distinct feeling that Alkali could part a gnat's hair with his, but it would pass the time and perhaps bring these two men closer. Morgan felt that any freight hauling to be done for de Lopez·into Mexico he would want done under the direction of Alkali Dakis.

Rattlesnake Run proved to be everything Alkali had claimed. Even moving slowly, a man would have been hard pressed to count the snakes basking in the sun. They were easy prey and taking one out in no way disturbed the others. Morgan surprised even himself with his accuracy. By the end of the first mile, he was in a dead heat tie—seven snakes apiece.

"You're pretty good with that thing, sonny. How 'bout we throw in a chunk o' beef steak an' some 'taters just to sweeten the pot a mite?"

"Why not?" Morgan said. Alkali shouted, cracked his whip and the team lurched forward—adding perhaps a third again the speed. Morgan frowned and looked at the older teamster. "You making it tougher, are you?"

"Stakes is higher." Alkali turned, grinned and said, "You go first this time." A large, flat rock lay just ahead. There were three snakes on it. Morgan's whip swished through the air behind him. The wagon approached, Morgan eyed his target and snapped his wrists as his right arm arced through the air above his head. The first rattler's head came off clean. Morgan smiled, pulled back his whip and coiled it for the next time.

"Your go, Alkali." Ahead, perhaps three quarters of a mile, Morgan could see the half dome boulder—the end of the run.

"Looks like a likely target just up there on the left," Alkali said. He was pointing. Morgan looked. Three snakes were coiled on a large rock and a fourth on a smaller rock just below it. Morgan was about to ask which target Alkali would select when the old man's blacksnake cut through the air. It was a little heavier weave than Morgan's. Morgan's whip, as Alkali phrased it, was "store bought." Alkali's was hand woven. Probably, so said the old teamster, by the "Apache" he killed to get it.

Morgan's face turned ashen as he watched Dakis work the end of that whip. He'd laid it behind him only once and now controlled it with short, crisp movements of his gnarled hand. One head—two—three—the last snake head flipped into the air and Alkali's whip came to rest behind him, in the wagon box.

"You're down by three, sonny. Not too fur to go, neither. I'd reckon you'll hav to take out three at one lick an' one at another if'n you figger to win our wager."

Morgan tried. Had he been wielding a six-gun, Alkali would have already lost. Try as might, he could not do better than one head per try. The increased speed took away any chance for catching up. Morgan had been "green-horned."

"I figured you to be a lot better than you let on," Morgan said, grinning, "but I didn't plan on looking foolish."

"Best advice I can give you, sonny," Alkali replied, "is don't never take on more'n one rattler at a time an' you'll be just fine!"

Morgan dozed off in the back of the wagon for a time. Alkali was pushing the team to make the trip, deadhead, in two days. He finally pulled the team up, well after sunset, in a shallow spot just off the road.

"What did we make today?" Morgan inquired.

"Nigh on to forty mile. We can lay easy on the team tomorrow an' still make the Pass by afternoon."

"Good driving, Alkali. Damned good."

"Thanky, sonny. Allus nice to hear good words about yourself now an' ag'in."

"Damn it's hot!"

"Yes sir—that it be. Have to side with that there gen'rul what said if'n he owned Texas and hell he'd live in hell an' rent Texas out."

"To who?"

"I don't recollect he ever got that far in his figgerin'," Alkali said, grinning. "But it'd sure be to some Texican. Fella don't narry tell that story to a Texican. Li'ble to come away shy a tooth or two."

."I take it you're not a Texican. Where are you from, Alkali?" Morgan busied himself fixing coffee as he talked. Alkali unharnessed the team and prepared to tether them for the night.

"No Texas man but I can't rightly say where I'm from. Seems to me, when I turned old enough to know where I was—and who—I was here in Texas. Been here ever since."

"Your people never talked about where they came from?"

"Didn't live long enough to talk to me. Comanche' kilt 'em. Two brothers an' a sister too." Alkali walked over to the fire and poured himself a cup of coffee. He blew, touched his tongue to the liquid, nodded his approval and then sipped. He continued. "Only thing saved me was a nor'easter. Leastways, the folks on the wagon train what come on me—they tol' me that later. Folks name o' Dakis took me in. Raised me 'til I turned twelve. Started mule skinnin' 'bout then. Been to it ever since."

"How'd they know you were twelve? Find anything with your people?"

"Nothin' left. Mizz Dakis figgered from muh teeth," Alkali guffawed. "Just like a goddam horse. Actual—don't rightly know how old I am. Just as soon not. Man starts thinkin' 'bout how old he is—he starts thinkin' 'bout how little he's got done. That there grates on 'im an' he starts tryin' to make up fer lost time. Tryin' to do that, he gits right down careless. Usual, that ends up gittin' him kilt an' he goes buhfore his time."

Morgan chuckled. It was what his dad had called "pot-belly philosophizing" but there was more than a little truth to it. Morgan scooped himself and Alkali a plate of beans. As he handed the plate to the old teamster, Alkali's eyes fixed on Morgan's face, he kept grinning and then spoke through clenched teeth.

"Keep lookin', keep actin' simple—we got company, Morgan. On foot. Two—mebbe three of 'em. Muh rifle's still in the wagon. Seems like you'll have to count on that handgun."

"More coffee," Morgan said, more loudly than necessary.

"Yep."

"When I holler," Morgan said, softly, "go flat and roll to your left toward the wagon." Alkali nodded as he tipped his head to drain his coffee cup. *"Now!"*

Sparks flew into the darkness as bullets ripped into the fire. Alkali rolled left and then, on hands and knees, scrambled beneath the big freight wagon. Morgan rolled right, drawing and firing at the flashes of gunpowder from their would-be murderers' guns. Far off, a horse whinnied—then another. Alkali had been right. Three men. One had stayed with their mounts.

Once again, Lee Morgan's accuracy had been unfailing. One man was dead. The other would be by sunup. The vastness of the desert soon swallowed up the sounds of the gunfire. Both Morgan and Alkali remained stone dead still.

Alkali and Morgan discussed the attack well into the night and most of the next day. Their arrival in Eagle Pass, about mid-afternoon, seemed quite a surprise to the owner of the small firm with whom they had contracted. Their business done, they repaired to *señora* Gordo's in order to afford Morgan the opportunity to make good on his wager. It was not long until Alkali had fallen in with a woman about half his age.

Morgan, amused by the old teamster's audacity, whiled away his time in a poker game.

He had just completed another winning hand when Alkali suddenly appeared at the table.

"You and I had best palaver." Morgan looked up. Alkali appeared stern.

"Trouble?"

" 'Fore we left today, I poked around out there in the desert, checkin' horse tracks. Mostly, I was wantin' to know if'n them mounts was shod or not."

Morgan got to his feet, picked up his winnings and said his farewells. The two men strode toward the bar. "Indians?"

"Not hardly. Mexican ponies most likely but I found one odd track. One horse with no shoe on a right foreleg."

"Whiskey," Morgan said to the barkeep.

"Same fer me."

"And," Morgan said.

"I heard a fella talkin' upstairs—to a gal. Said he didn't have much time. Said his horse was gittin' one shot put on so she'd have to be quick about her business."

"You see this fella?"

"Nope—but I wandered down to the smithy. He's got a little chestnut mare down there. Four white stockings. She's missin' a front shoe—right foreleg."

"Stay put," Morgan said. He downed his whiskey and pushed away from the bar. "I'll introduce myself to our friend."

"Can't be sure he's still by hisself."

"That's why I want you here. If he's got friends you'll have the best chance of spotting them."

Alkali nodded. "Watch yourself."

"You too."

Morgan found the blacksmith busy. The man didn't look up when Morgan began to talk. "I'm looking for the man that owns a chestnut mare with a missing shoe on her right front leg."

"My job's shoein', mister, not keepin' track of who owns 'em."

"Just thought you might know where I could find this gent."

"Well—I don't."

"You looking for me, little man?" Morgan whirled. He saw one of the biggest men he'd ever seen. He was well over six and a half feet and must have weighed near 275 pounds. It was not fat.

"If you're one of three who shot at me last night—yeah," Morgan said, "I'm looking for you." The man grinned.

"Well, mister, you're luck's done run out—'cause you went and found me." On that word, the man lunged at Morgan. He was fast, surprisingly so for his size. He caught Morgan with a backhand swing which struck the gunman's upper shoulder but the force was enough to take Morgan off his feet. He rolled and came up in a crouch. The man swung and Morgan ducked, moving in and throwing to quick, solid punches to the man's mid-section. They were totally without effect. Morgan danced away. They circled one another, warily.

A crowd had gathered. Apparently the big man spotted Morgan, knew who he was and made one reference or another to how Morgan would end up. The blacksmith stepped between the two. He was holding a shotgun, its hammers cocked.

"I got a business here and I don't figure to have it busted up by the likes o' you two. Move outside and settle your differences." The big man moved toward him, menacingly. "Big as you are, mister—this scatter gun 'll make an awful nasty hole in your belly." The big man stopped. "And," the blacksmith added, "I'll trouble you for what you owe me just in case this gent with the fast draw rig decides to even up the fight some."

"I'll settle with you personal, smithy, when I'm finished with *him.*" The big man was pointing at Morgan with one hand and pulling money from his pocket with the other. He tossed some bills toward the blacksmith. The smithy picked up two of them, never letting his eyes leave the big man.

"I won't try you bare-handed, mister. I'll just blow your goddam head off if you come back here lookin' for trouble. Now git!"

The big man pushed several people aside so that he might block Morgan's exit and, if the gunman was so inclined, his escape route. Morgan wasn't so inclined, but he was fully aware of the trouble he faced.

"Now little man—I'm about to break you in half." The man wasn't wearing a gun or a knife or any weapon that Morgan could see. He'd learned long ago that pulling a gun on an unarmed man, no matter how outclassed he was, brought quick retaliation from the onlookers.

Morgan charged, head down, bull-like, into the man's middle. This time, there was a grunt and the man reeled backwards a few steps. But he did not go down. Instead, his huge arms encircled Morgan's chest, slipping beneath the gunman's arms. He lifted. Morgan came up. The man slammed him down and Morgan's knees buckled. Now, the hulking antagonist locked his fingers and began tightening his grip. Morgan knew the bear hug would take all the breath out of him and, once that was done, begin to crack ribs.

While the big man laughed and squeezed Morgan tried everything. First, he tried to butt the man's nose with his forehead. The big man simply turned his head sideways. Then, Morgan worked his hands up and tried to lever the man's head backwards by applying pressure under the man's chin.

"Jeezus," Morgan whispered to himself. The man's neck was like a wagon axle. "Uhhhnuh!" The man tightened the grip, lifted Morgan's feet from the ground and whirled around several times. Morgan's body felt like a rag doll. His boot toes dragged in the dirt and finally, the man stopped. Morgan was dizzy. His eyes scanned the crowd and finally fell upon Alkali. There was a man next to him—holding a pistol on him.

Morgan's breath was being forced from his body in increasingly large doses. The constriction would soon be against a rib cage with nothing inside to bolster its resistance. The man whirled Morgan again and again, the gunman could see Alkali's face. This time, the old teamster closed both hands into fists, extended his index fingers and quickly moved them to his ears. Morgan was whirled again and gasped the last of his air out.

"Now, little man, let's see what you're made of." The giant's hands slipped apart for the smallest part of a second. Then his right fingers closed around his left wrist. The crushing hold was locked into place. In a great heave, Morgan stretched his body back as far as he could. The move surprised the big man and he turned his face toward Morgan's. At that moment, Morgan's hands, fingers tight together and palms curved into little cups, shot upwards and out, away from the man's head. Like cymbals, they came back toward one another —closing finally over the man's ears.

The man howled in pain, released his grip, staggered backwards and his own hands shot up, covering his own ears as though the action would stop the pain and the ringing. Morgan was through with Marquis of Queensbury rules. His right foot lashed out, the toe of his boot landed, dead center, in the man's groin. The hulk, still holding his ears, screamed, leaned forward and then dropped to his knees. His hands came away from his ears and he flailed them, blindly, in front of him. Morgan deftly dodged his efforts, stepped inside the man's reach and, using the butt of his hand, swinging it in an upward arc, struck the base of the man's nose. He heard the bone crack. He felt the initial pressure give way. Morgan stepped back. The man's eyes rolled back in his head, blood spurted, in a needle-fine stream, from where his nose had been. His mouth opened, he teetered for just a moment and then fell, face down. He didn't move. The nose bone had been driven into the brain. The giant was dead!

"Son-of-a-bitch!" The man holding the gun on Alkali could scarcely believe what he had just witnessed. Once the realization had registered, he stepped back, raised his weapon and heard a shot. Morgan's pistol had come out of nowhere. The shot killed the man instantly.

"Clear out," Morgan shouted, uncertain as to the crowd's intentions or whether it secreted more of the big man's allies. He fired a shot into the air and another into the dirt near those closest to him. He got the desired effect and the crowd dispersed quickly. They were replaced by a U.S. marshal and a deputy.

"I'll have your gun, mister, till I can sort things out." Morgan moved back a few steps.

"Turn it over," Alkali said. "This here's a fair man an' we don't need no troubles with the law."

"Alkali—I didn't see you there. You in on this?"

"Indirect like, Marshal."

"You know this gent?"

"I know 'im." Alkali turned to Morgan. "This here is the Territorial Marshal, Cass Breymer. Cass, meet Lee Morgan."

Alkali Dakis and Lee Morgan accompanied the marshal and his deputy back to the Eagle Pass jail. There, after more than an hour, they learned the identities of the two men who had very nearly done them in. Alkali's tormentor was known to the law only as Logan. He was a sometime bounty hunter with a less than honorable reputation. The none too gentle giant who nearly ended Morgan's life was Reed Loftus.

"Now we know who," Morgan said, nodding to the marshal and smiling as he returned Morgan's gun, "but the more important question is *why*?"

"You spell trouble," Cass Breymer said, "and the answer to the first question tells me all I need to know about the second one. These trail tramps were on a Mexican payroll. I'd guess their wages came direct from Mexico City."

"Anti-revolution?"

"I'd wager on it."

Morgan didn't like what he was hearing. It spelled more trouble than he'd been led to believe by de Lopez. And it was trouble that Luke and Lucy Masters were hardly ready to handle. "How do you see this Mexican business shaping up, Marshal?"

"Bloody and long." Cass Breymer fired up a cheroot, took a long drag, let the smoke squeeze between his lips and then said, "For me—and Texas—the fella headin' up this revolution against the Mexican government is no damn better than they are. I've got a hunch that if he should win, he'd be a hell of a lot worse."

"Any move to stop him?"

"You mean from our side. From our government?" Morgan nodded. Breymer grinned and shook his head. "The last thing we'll do is interfere in the affairs of the Mexicans. Hasn't been that many years ago that we whipped 'em, Morgan. We mess into it now—we may end up havin' both bunches take into us. We won't do a thing."

Breymer got to his feet. "I got business elsewhere, Mr. Morgan, but if you'll heed a little advice, I'd stay out of the business south o' here." Breymer waggled a finger at Alkali. "That goes for you too, you old desert rat."

"I'll think on it, Marshal," Morgan said. He extended his hand and Breymer shook it. "Maybe next time we cross trails I can buy you a drink."

"I'd like that, Morgan. Maybe you could tell me a few facts about the old days—you know—set things straight for me." He smiled and held up a copy of the latest edition of "Deadwood Dick's" dime novel adventure. "Read one o' these recent about Buckskin Frank Leslie."

Morgan grinned. "Which one? Where he killed the grizzly bare handed or fought twenty Sioux to a stand-

still with a single shot Sharps and a Bowie knife?"
Breymer laughed.

Walking back to the livery barn, Morgan was quiet. It
was obvious he was deeply concerned over the commit-
ment to de Lopez. By the time he and Alkali got there,
Morgan had made a decision.

Inside, Alkali hitched up the team, all the while
eyeing Morgan who was checking the bill of lading
against the load. When he finished the last of the hitch
work, Alkali turned to Morgan and said, "You might
convince ol' man Masters to get out o' that Mexican
deal, but Miss Lucy'll fight you tooth an' nail." Alkali
grinned. "She'll make that Goliath you tangled with
today look like a preachin' man."

"Yeah," Morgan said. "I know. They need the
money. Real bad."

"I don't mind makin' the run alone," Alkali said.
"Been doin' it fer more years than I care to count."

"You one o' them *seers,* Alkali, like I've heard old
P.T. Barnum talk about?"

Alkali grinned. "I don't find much miracle 'bout a
gent that understands another gent's thinkin'."

"You haven't known me that long."

"Saw what you did. Heard why. Heard you say what
bothered you. Don't need no more'n that to make muh
judgin'. Ride on out. You'll git to Uvalde by noon
tomorrow if'n you don't get jumped or shot along the
way. I'll be behind—an' not too far neither."

"I still owe you a steak dinner. You'd better show up
and collect it," Morgan said, saddling his horse. "If
you don't, you forfeit."

"Sure wouldn't want to do that. Don't figger to

sucker you into many more wagerin' contests." The two men shook hands. Morgan didn't let on just how concerned he was for Alkali's safety. It was a long, lonely and dangerous trip from Hell to Uvalde. Or, Morgan thought to himself, was it the other way 'round?

7

Morgan's hell-bent-for-leather ride back to Uvalde was uneventful save for the workings of his own imagination. He was trying to conjure up some reasonable argument to deter the Masters from honoring their contract with de Lopez. He had also reached the conclusion that whoever was raiding the area's ranches—including the big and powerful Double C—might also be responsible for crippling—or attempting to cripple—the local freight outfits. Success in these two areas would leave an open field of operation for someone.

As Alkali had predicted, Morgan arrived in Uvadle just before noon. He felt a twinge of concern when he rode up in front of the Masters' home. There were nearly a dozen mounts tethered outside. One of them he recognized. It belonged to Charity Coltrane.

"Morgan?" Lucy answered the door and registered surprise, almost shock, at seeing him. "Where's Alkali?" The question carried a tone of concern and she looked past him as she asked it.

"He's bringing the load—somewhere behind me. He'll be okay." Lucy stepped back and Morgan entered the living room. He saw many strange faces and a few he recognized.

"Morgan rode back ahead of our load from Eagle Pass, Dad," Lucy said. Then, she turned to the others. "This is Lee Morgan. He hired on as our shotgun rider." She frowned and looked back at Morgan. "Alkali is out there alone. Why?" Morgan detected a slight change in the tone of her voice. Now, Lucy Masters was playing boss lady.

"Somebody tried us on the way down. Two men tried us after we got to our destination. They're both dead. The marshal told us they were working for the Mexican government. You've got some mighty powerful enemies aligned against you, and apparently they've already heard about your contract with de Lopez." Morgan looked right at Luke Masters. "If you take my advice you'll back off. Drop that contract. It'll buy you more trouble than you can handle."

"It will leave us bankrupt if we don't take it," Lucy said, scathingly.

"It may leave you dead if you do," Morgan retorted.

"Is that why you came back ahead of Alkali? You want to talk us out of the best contract we've ever had?"

"Lucy," Luke Masters said, "I don't think Morgan is trying to undermine us." He turned to face Morgan. "I'd like to hear more. What else do you know?"

"Nothing yet."

"And with nothing you ask us to back out?"

"Look. You sent me to San Antonio to negotiate. You told me before I left that you weren't too inclined to get mixed up in a revolution. Well—I know more now than I did when I made the deal. Not much more but enough that—well, if I'd known it then—I'd have turned the deal down.''

"Maybe," Lucy said. "But we know more too and with what we know I'd have taken it or ordered you to take it. Maybe you'd best hear from some of these other folks."

Charity Coltrane took the floor. As she looked at Morgan, her thoughts darted back to the privacy of her bedroom and the image of herself, nude, eyes closed and Morgan's hands on her, instead of her own. She felt her cheeks getting warm and tingly. She tried to hide the reaction, imagining it to be more obvious than it really was.

"The ranchers represented in this room have agreed to band together. They want to form a coalition for protection of one another and protection of a freight supply line in and out of Uvalde which can serve them all." Charity, as she had spoken, had turned her back on Morgan. Now, she felt under control and turned to face him. "We too have some new information. If it's accurate, it places a whole new light on the situation hereabouts."

"I'm pleased for you," Morgan said, looking first at Charity and then glancing from face to face around the room, "but I fail to see what that has to do with the Masters or their contract with the Mexicans."

"If what we know is correct, Mr. Morgan, it has everything to do with it. We have reason to believe that my—my bastard brother is back in Texas and is responsible for the recent raids." Morgan looked surprised, then quizzical. "We've had four reports in the past two days about him." She half smiled. "We know it wasn't you they saw this time."

"All right," Morgan said, walking across the room to where he could get himself a cup of coffee, "I'll admit to considering the possibility of raids on both the ranches and the freight line being done by the same gang." He poured a cup of coffee, sipped it twice, turned and then continued. "Given that it is Marshall Coltrane, what connection do you make with de Lopez or the revolution?"

"That's what we intend to find out, Mr. Morgan."

"And we want *you* to do it," Lucy interjected.

"Whoa! I hired on as a shotgun rider for a freight line. I'm not Pinkerton man."

"You have been." Morgan eye-balled the speaker. A thin faced, bearded man, wearing an expensive looking, store bought suit. "Jason Smithers, Mr. Morgan, Cattleman's Bank and Trust Company. San Antonio."

"I did some work for the Pinkertons but I'm not now —and I don't intend to."

"I didn't mean to infer that you should, sir, only that you have the kind of experience we need in this thing and you've already made some of the contacts."

"If you're what you claim and you know so damned much about me, I'd think you be pretty well up on one Mexican named de Lopez."

"I am. Frankly, it's my own opinion that Miss Coltrane's somewhat dubious kin and his cutthroats are working for the other side."

Morgan cocked his head. "The Mexican government? Anti-revolutionary?"

"Exactly!"

"What makes you think so?"

"You're a tracker of men, Mr. Morgan, and a good one as I hear it. Me? I'm a tracker of money, also a good one. I've tracked money, considerable amounts of it, through several Mexican and south Texas banks. The trail leads back to the Mexican government. The revolutionary faction, headed up by young Pancho Villa, has very few sources of funds. Right now his primary one, and his largest, is de Lopez, here in Texas, not in Mexico.''

"I can add a little to the theory," Charity said. "Marsh Coltrane was always an evil man. I've no reason to think he's changed any. He's greedy, selfish, uncaring about anyone but himself and totally without principles. He was also flat broke. In spite of everything else about him, Marsh is no small thinker. He wouldn't even consider petty stage holdups—train robberies or bank jobs.''

"But a revolution—that he'd go for?"

Charity smiled. "Sure, Morgan, as long as he could keep his own hide out of the line of fire. This gang of raiders is very tricky. They're good—professional. Now Marsh is a leader. But he could never have financed such an outfit on his own.''

"So what we have in Marsh Coltrane—or whoever it is—is something of a poor man's Bill Quantrill—out to fill his own pocket.''

"I'd say that was a fair assessment, Mr. Morgan."

"You agree, Charity?"

"I do. One more thing too. Rest assured that Marsh will keep himself right down the middle on this thing. If he comes to believe he's on the losing side, he'll jump the fence in an instant.''

Morgan looked around the room. Most of the faces had shown little change in expression since his arrival. Now, each seemed a bit apprehensive. These were not gunmen or revolutionaries or political activists. These people were citizens, in business and trying to build a future, their own and that of yet unborn generations, amid a wild and dangerous environment. They had sacrificed much and asked little in return.

"All right, gentlemen and ladies," Morgan said, "you want to band together and stand against the wrongs that are being thrust upon you—very noble. Now let's look at a few facts. You have one line of supply, already strained to the limit and subject to almost total destruction with only one more raid. I give you the Masters Cartage Company of Uvalde, Texas."

Morgan returned his coffee cup to the small serving tray and moved, instead, to a nearby stand which held a variety of harder stuff. He poured a healthy measure of Tennessee mash, downed about half of it and then turned back to his audience.

"Mr. Morgan—I—" Morgan held up his hand.

"Just a moment more," he said, "please. As I was saying, the Masters here are your single supply line. Assuming they survive whoever has been striking at them, they have a questionable contract to haul goods for a known supporter of a revolution which, by its leader's own admission, is sometime off yet." Morgan finished off the Tennessee mash, walked over, refilled his glass and held up his arm in the manner of a long-winded legislator about to embark on a campaign speech. "Finally, we have a gang of professional gunmen, led by a lunatic, with loyalties in direct proportion to the fattest purse available." Morgan again downed the remainder of the whiskey in his glass, refilled it and turned back to the crowd. He hadn't eaten, he was tired and tense, a little disgusted, in part with himself, and bent on getting rip-roaring drunk, no matter the outcome of the meeting.

"Mr. Morgan, I believe, sir, you're beginning to feel the effects of that whiskey. Perhaps we should resume this meeting at some other time."

"I haven't had the pleasure, sir," Morgan said, half bowing to the speaker whose name he didn't know. "Nonetheless, a toast to your success." Morgan emptied the glass. Lucy Masters moved toward him. He glowered at her. Charity caught the look and stifled a snicker. She knew what a man had to do sometimes, and Morgan, without any doubt in her mind, was all man. Morgan downed another glass of mash. "I'll work for you," he said. "I'll find out just who is on whose side and why." He smiled. "I give you my word as a gentleman." He chuckled, "And as a gunman, scoundrel, sometimes gambler and womanizer."

He straightened to his full height, tipped his head back and drained the glass one more time. He wiped his mouth, looked at each person in the room for a moment and said, in his most serious tone, "And I will begin my duties officially, at sometime just past midday tomorrow." Lee Morgan was well on his way to one of the biggest binges he'd been on for many a year.

Lucy Masters, somewhat embarrassed, stood by the door and thanked each of the visiting ranchers. She was grateful that their wives had not accompanied them. One, John Findlay, a somewhat stiff necked, moral zealot, made the only comment about Morgan.

"I'm not certain, Miss Masters, that the man you have suggested to us is at all the man we want for the job." Charity Coltrane was within earshot and moved to rebut Findlay's observation. She found no need and gained a new and what would become lasting respect for Lucy Masters.

Lucy looked up at the straight-laced Findlay, smiled and said, "I quite agree with you, Mr. Findlay, that Morgan may not be the man we want. But having witnessed the male members of the ranchers' association here gathered today I am quite convinced he is the man we need!"

Everyone went home—everyone but Charity Coltrane. She watched Morgan make his way to the hotel saloon and casino. There, he spent more than six hours drinking and playing poker. He consumed far more whiskey than he won money, but he was surprisingly alert when he finally quit the establishment. It was nearing dark.

"Morgan!" He turned, muscles tense, obviously prepared for the worst. "You seem quite able to hold your liquor."

"It only takes one hand," he said, smiling at Charity. Then, he looked a little puzzled by her presence. "In my business you never completely drop your guard."

"Come home with me," she said.

"Why?"

"I need—to talk."

"I've had a belly full of talking since I've been in Texas and more than enough for today. Besides, I'm worried about Alkali."

"Don't be. He pulled in two hours ago. He's fine. So is the shipment. He's at the Masters' place now. If you go there you'll just have more talk." She smiled—a different smile—a woman's smile.

"And if I go home with you?"

"We'll do our talking on the way. It's near twelve miles."

"And a long ride back."

"I've got plenty of room."

The Double C ranch was everything Morgan had imagined it would be. Where Charity Coltrane herself was concerned, Morgan found his imagination lacking. The reality was breathtaking. Morgan was relaxing on the swan's down mattress and eyeing the trappings in the bedroom of a once wealthy, female Texas cattle ranch owner. Charity entered the room, moving across it on the balls of her feet. She was clad only in an unfastened, silk robe.

At the bed's edge, she dropped the robe, reached to the top of her head and removed two combs. The movement caused her breasts to sway and Morgan followed the movement, licking his lips. He was not certain that his action was prompted by his anticipation or the thirst brought about by too much Tennessee mash. He didn't care.

"You smell good," he said, as Charity leaned down and kissed him. Morgan moved over and Charity slipped beneath the covers beside him. They kissed.

Charity Coltrane conducted business with the cold calculations of a railroad president, used Colt .45's with the skill of a gunfighter, usually dressed like a wrangler and most of the time spoke like a lady. She made love like a whore.

She seemed to know every movement to make and just when to make it. She explored Morgan's body first. Fingers touched, teased and moved on. She was familiarizing herself with the terrain, becoming knowledgable enough to assure her partner's satisfaction. Lee Morgan was letting her. Then, it was his turn.

Charity's breasts were large, pendulous, somewhat pear shaped and, Morgan discovered, highly sensitive. She lapsed into a state resembling a trance each time he fondled them. His fingers kneaded and worked the pliant flesh, stroking and lightly pinching the pink, hardened tips. He slipped lower and closed his lips, gently, over one of them.

"Don't stop," she whispered. It was a breathless mandate, punctuated with a grinding of her hips into Morgan's groin. He knew he would have to concentrate to avoid a premature conclusion to their lovemaking. He did.

As their roles had reversed, Morgan found that there was barely a few square inches of Charity's flesh which was not responsive to his touch. She moaned once or twice, but most of the time only the sound of her heavy breathing and the occasional soft, sucking noises of Morgan's mouth could be heard.

When he reached the very heart of her sexual being, he mentally noted the exceptional softness of her pubic hair.

"Wait!" He was puzzled. Charity placed her hands on either side of his head and pushed him away, gently. Her hands slipped from his face and disappeared into the darkness. "Now," she said, "do it now." Morgan lowered his head. She had placed her hands in such a manner as to allow her to use her fingers to spread herself even wider. The act seemed to increase her own passion but if it did not, Morgan's movements did. His own hands free, he reached above him and began to caress her breasts again.

Thrice, Charity Coltrane's body stiffened. The third time the action was so violent she nearly bucked Morgan off. Just as suddenly, she gripped his shoulders and pushed, hard, forcing him to his knees. Nonetheless, her expertise in making requests without speaking was amazing. She led. Morgan followed. They blended as though they had enjoyed each other's desires hundreds of times.

Morgan rolled over, lay on his back and Charity straddled him. She used her hands to guide his throbbing, swollen tool into the passion soaked depths of her womanhood. Even their movements needed no rehearsal. Their timing and bodies melded into a single motion. Morgan's head was swimming with pleasure and his groin filled to the bursting point with his own passion.

"Ooh—ooh, ooh God!" Charity almost screamed when, at last, they came together in an explosive moment which drained them both. Morgan heard his own sounds. Guttural groans of total satisfaction. This was not an act of reproduction or human passion cleaned and polished by two people in love. This was raw, physical sex.

"You're the best I've ever had," Morgan said, a few minutes later. They were still side by side in the dark. He heard her little chuckle.

"I find that hard to believe. A man like you? It's nice to hear, of course, for any woman, but hard to believe."

"Yeah," Morgan agreed, "I find it hard to believe I

said it, but it doesn't change a damn thing. It's a fact."

She raised up on her elbows and looked at him. She really couldn't see him that well. It was too dark. Still, she looked. "You mean it, don't you?"

"You think I have to pay tribute to every woman I bed down? Hell—most men only do that because they think words are as important to women as actions. I give what I've got—take what there is in return and we both walk away. If we're both a little happier for it, that's reward enough. I don't have to talk about it."

Charity wanted to talk about it. She wanted to whisper in his ear how good she thought he was, and how she would want him again—soon! She didn't. Such talk from her would have ruined it. Instead, she kissed him. Then, Charity slipped from the bed, washed and put on a nightgown. By then, Lee Morgan was sound asleep.

8

Several things had to happen all at once. Even if he'd had the time, Morgan couldn't spread himself that thin, and he didn't have the time. He was no more than dressed the following morning when Charity summoned him downstairs. Jed Railsback was there. So was Jimmy Willow. He was the son of Bert and Olive Willow, two of the staunchest supporters of Charity's plan to fight back.

Morgan was still tucking in his shirttail as he came down the stairs. He could see by the look on Charity's face that something was wrong.

"Trouble?"

"Tell 'im, Jed."

"Mebbe Jimmy here could tell 'im better'n me."

"They hit our place last night, 'bout midnight. Twenty—twenty-five of 'em. Burned most o' the out buildin's an' what stock they couldn't run off they shot. Lost six men. That many more run off. They've had enough fightin'."

Morgan looked from the boy's face to Jed's and then to Charity's.

"Jimmy Willow," Charity said, pouring two cups of coffee and then pointing to a third cup while glancing at Jed. He nodded. "You met his daddy, at least briefly."

"Yeah." Morgan looked back at the boy. "Your folks make it?" He nodded. "Will they stick?"

"I don't think so. Can't without hands. Nobody'll be able to git'ny help soon. Might be too late already."

"Who were these night raiders, Jimmy?"

"You *know* damned well who they were," Charity snapped. She handed Morgan a cup of hot coffee. He looked into her eyes. Where was the Charity Coltrane of a few hours ago? The breathless, passion-filled woman? A man, he thought, just tucked his dick back between his legs like he'd holster his six-gun. Loaded and ready for use the next time. A woman seemed to change bodies. Minds, anyway.

"No, Charity," he said, "we don't know for sure and until we do, it's damned stupid to make our moves on a wrong assumption."

"What the hell difference does it make? Even if it isn't, Marsh, people are just as scared, runnin' off just as quick, or just as dead."

"You're right," Morgan agreed, shaking his head and blowing on the hot coffee, "as far as you go with it, but it makes a hell of a lot of difference in how we handle it."

"How so?"

"If it's Marshall Contrane, he won't quit 'til he's dead or he's won. Somebody else might. Too, if the gang is being grubstaked by the Mexican government— then they're going to have to show results. So far they really haven't done much, but if it's Marsh, then he could have promised the Mexicans a solid base of operations against Lopez and Villa, a base right here in Texas." Charity looked up, her eyebrows raised. She hadn't considered that possibility.

"You mean," she said, pointing at the floor, "*here*—the Double C." Morgan nodded.

"There's one way to find out—*positive*," she said, standing up.

"How?" Morgan asked, tentatively.

"I'll put the word out that I want to talk."

"He'll kill you, Miss Charity," Jed said. " 'Bout as fast as he would me, or Morgan here."

"Faster maybe," Morgan said.

"Not the first time around he won't. After that it won't make a damn."

"The answer is *no*!"

"You don't give me orders, Morgan. And if you did I wouldn't follow them."

"Don't go emotional on me," Morgan shot back. "I need time to do some snooping and try to pull together a few men, find out who'll stand and who won't."

"An' those what will are thinnin' out ever'day," Jed said. "Ma'am, he's right."

Charity whirled and jammed her index finger into the air—right straight at Jed Railsback. "You do work for me, Jed—so you'd best remember that I give the orders on the Double C."

Morgan got his fill. He said, "Fine, lady, you do it and you damn well better enjoy it 'cause I got a gut feeling you won't have the chance very much longer."

Whether or not the meek shall inherit the earth remains a matter of conjecture, but here and now they must be credited with having already inherited their share of common sense. Young Jimmy Willow spoke up.

"Whoever's leadin' that gang out there has already got us whipped. He's got us fightin' ag'in our own-selves. All's he's gotta do is wait 'til ever'body splits up an' then move in an' kill what's left."

Eyes met. Morgan's and Charity's. Charity's and Jed's. Jed's and Morgan's. Six eyes evenly distributed, Morgan thought, among three fools and not a damned one of them could see past the end of his own nose.

"The boy is right." This from Charity. If she wasn't the first to think it, she was the first to express it. Morgan just nodded. Jed Railsback spoke up.

"Folks around here find out they got nobody to lead 'em—they'll back off fast." He turned to Morgan. "You said you needed time to snoop around an' then try to pull some men together. Way I see it—you snoop you won't get many answers. Even if'n you do, they'll prob'ly be too late to do us any good. Far as men are concerned—none hereabouts'll follow you—leastways not right now."

"Yeah, Jed, you're makin' as a good sense as young Willow here. Trouble is they're questions. Not answers. Got any of those?"

"Mebbe."

"Shoot."

"Well—thinkin' about it instead o' worryin'—Miss Charity's idea makes sense. Right now, even if it's Marshall Coltrane, they's no connection between you'n her. You're s'posed to be workin' for the Masters'."

"So far so good."

"So Miss Charity sets up a meetin'. If'n it is Marshall he'll be plumb curious. Even settin' it up could take a few days, mebbe even a week. That'd buy you some o' that time."

"And if it isn't Marshall Coltrane?"

"Then whoever it is don't seem likely to bother."

"He's right," Charity said. Morgan eyed her. There was that change in expression again. A look of confidence, hope—not hate and revenge. Those kinds of motives, Morgan knew all too well, could get you dead in a hurry. "If it is Marsh, I could even stretch the time out a little, delay by a day or two what he wants." Now she was warming to the subject. She poured more coffee. "Jed could handle things in this territory. He knows damned near every working hand in fifty miles. He could soon find out which ones got backbone."

"An' I could help too. I think my daddy might if'n he knowed there was a chance to win."

"There are a few other owners around like Jimmy's dad too. Men who are respected. Hell, with each ranch contributing even four or five guns, we could put together a small army."

"And if you're found out—whether it's Marsh or not —then what?"

"Then," Charity said, looking Morgan straight in the eye, "I'd be dead." She smiled and added, "Which I'd rather be than run off. I'm sure you can't understand that, Morgan, just how much a ranch can mean."

Morgan smiled, sardonically, at Charity's final observation. His thoughts shot back to Idaho and the burned out remnants of the Spade Bit. He shook his head to clear away the memories. He looked at Charity. He'd tell her. Sometime—somewhere—he'd tell her. Not here. Not now.

"Okay," he said. "It's Marshall Coltrane and you've

got a meeting. Then what?''

"For one thing, I can get a pretty damned good idea of just how many men he's actually got. For another, I can make him a deal with the ranch. He'll have to wait long enough to find out if I'm serious. By the time he learned the truth—well—by then we'd better be ready.''

"And one way we might be ready is for me to talk to our Mexican friends again. If we can get the freight wagons moving to Mexico—and you're talking a deal with Marsh Coltrane—he'll have to keep an eye in both directions—and men.''

"I'll git on to town an' start doin' some talkin'— lettin' the word spread.''

" 'Scuse me fer buttin' in ag'in,'' Jimmy Willow said, ''but it kinda seems to me that I oughta do the spreadin'. Might sound a little fishy comin' from a Double C hand. Particular the ramrod. What with our place bein' hit'n all, seems like them sidewinders would be more likely to believe what they're hearin' from somebody like me.''

Morgan was just finishing his coffee. He had to swallow fast to keep from choking. Then, he laughed. "You know, Jimmy, Charity here is by far the best lookin' one of this bunch. I'd wager there aren't any better wranglers anywhere in a day's ride than Jed and I'm more than a fair hand with a six-gun. I'm damned if I know where any of us would be without your brains.'' Everyone looked at everyone. Soon, they were all laughing.

Jesus de Lopez listened intently to Lee Morgan's report of activities around Uvalde. Morgan didn't hold back on the details and finally got to the agreement between Lopez and the Masters Cartage Company.

"You're got your own interests to protect in this deal," Morgan said. They'd been drinking wine. Quite a lot. Morgan wasn't through. His glass was empty and he eyed the bottle.

"Help yourself, Mr. Morgan." Morgan nodded. "I can supply guards to ride with each load. Extra riders too."

"Not enough you can't," Morgan replied, sipping at his fourth glass of wine. "Besides, to be blunt about it, there are questions as to just who these raiders might be working for. Your name hasn't been taken off of the list of possible employers."

"Surely, you don't believe they work for me?"

"What *I* believe doesn't have a damn thing to do with it. You want supplies taken into Mexico for Villa, then you'll have to assure protection. That will take more than a few riders."

"I—I don't understand, *señor.*"

"Simple. Quickest way for you to protect those shipments is to help wipe out the threat to them." Morgan's proposal hadn't been a part of any plan—his or anyone else's. On the ride from Uvalde, he kept pondering the problem of manpower to combat the raiders. He knew, at best, the ranchers might come up with fifteen or twenty men like Jed Railsback. They wouldn't be as good as what they were up against and —with somebody paying them handsomely—the ranch hands sure as hell wouldn't have the incentive of their opposition.

"*Señor,* you propose that I hire gunmen to fight these men?"

"Not at all. You've already got the manpower,

Villa.'' Jesus de Lopez suddenly lost his composure. He was shaking his head, negatively, even as he got to his feet.

"It is out of the question, Morgan. Completely out of the question.'' He turned away. "It was *not* part of the agreement we had before. It—well—it cannot be done.'' Morgan had expected some resistance, but nothing like he was getting. He was a little puzzled.

"Your refusal won't look so hot, Lopez, to a lot of people.'' Lopez turned around. "And *you, señor?* How does it look to you?''

"Frankly—awful goddam fishy.''

"You don't understand.''

"Then clarify it for me.''

Lopez paced. He sighed. He poured himself a glass of whiskey. He offered none. Again, he paced.

Lee Morgan had seen such discomfort in men before. Jesus de Lopez knew a hell of a lot more than he'd ever revealed—or something else was wrong. Morgan didn't intend to leave San Antonio until he found out what it was. He decided to wiggle the horns of the dilemma upon which Lopez was impaled.

" 'Course,'' he said, off-handedly, "there are other freight outfits in Texas.'' The comment brought unexpected results.

"You are trying to blackmail me, Morgan, and I don't like it. I could have you killed—here and now. No one would ask any questions. Even your friends in Uvalde would have to accept your death, given what happened the last time you were here.''

Now Morgan was really curious. Why was this wealthy Mexican so horn-swaggled by Morgan's proposal? After all, Morgan reasoned, it was to Lopez's advantage, more than anyone's, to protect those shipments once they began.

"*Señor* Lopez, what are you afraid of?"

Lopez stopped pacing. He looked into Morgan's face. "I fear nothing," he said. "And you will leave me now. I must think. We will speak again this evening." He moved to the door, opened it and stepped aside. Morgan considered resisting, but he might go too far too soon. Instead, he went to his room.

Morgan lay on the bed, one arm resting over his eyes. He wanted to doze off but his mind was reeling, considering every possibility of which he could conceive to explain Lopez's attitude. Too, on an only slightly lesser scale of importance, Morgan wondered about the whereabouts of Madiera. She was not at the *hacienda*. Nor had she been mentioned. A knock at the door brought Morgan's gun into his hand. He felt a little silly. His mind had been miles away from his surroundings. He had acted out of years of reflex.

"It's open." Maria Correra entered the room. Morgan sat up. He frowned. She was Madiera's handmaiden by Spanish standards. She was nervous. "Close it," Morgan said. She didn't move. "It's okay. Close it." She did. Then she stood again—almost frozen. Morgan suspected the had brought a message from Madiera but the more time that passed the less he believed it. "What is it?"

The woman, pleasant enough, Morgan recalled, began rattling in Mexican. He could catch only a word or two. He finally shook his head and held up his hand. *"Ingles?"*

"Si. You're too fast—uh—*rapido."* She nodded.

"Señor Lopez, he has *mucho desgracia. Señorita*

Madiera . . . she went—taken by *el malhechor*. He—
señor Lopez—he—he is—uh, *atemorezado.
Comprende?"*

Morgan shook his head. "Barely," he mumbled.
Loosely sorted out, he gathered that Madiera had gone
away with someone! Morgan's head jerked up. *"El
malehechor.* The evil one?" Maria nodded.

"Villa?"

"Si."

"Shit! He kidnapped her? Took her by force?"
Morgan put his own hands around his own throat to
demonstrate. Maria shook her head. "But," Morgan
added, "she didn't want to go, and Lopez didn't want
her to go."

Morgan, as best as he could, assured the frightened
Maria that her tale-carrying would be safe with him. He
sent her on her way and then made his own way back to
the library. Now, he found the big Mexican he'd met on
his first trip blocking the door.

"I need to see your boss," Morgan said, trying to
remember the man's name. It finally came to him.
"Enrique."

"You will not catch me as you did before, not again
señor." He'd out-drawn the Mexican. Made him look
bad in front of his boss. Now he didn't have time.

"I need to see *señor* Lopez."

"When *he* says."

Morgan smiled and shrugged, turned, spun back and
let go a full fledged haymaker that took Enrique off his
feet, onto the floor and into dreamland. Morgan walked
over him and opened the door. Lopez was halfway to it,
having heard the commotion outside. Morgan closed
the door.

"Don't call for anybody," Morgan said. "You don't need more trouble and neither do I. Sit down." He gave Lopez about three seconds. "Now!"

Lopez sat, his shoulders dropped and he rubbed his face with both hands. "I think you'd better tell me everything—for both our sakes."

"It's Villa. When I first agreed to help him he was different."

"A common man with a cause." Lopez looked somewhat surprised at Morgan's rather sudden grasp of the scenario. He didn't know that Morgan had seen scores of such men over the years. Often the taste of power was far more devastating to an otherwise sound man than was either whiskey or a woman. Even gold fever seemed pale by comparison. A man with power just out of reach will often destroy everything and everyone around him to get at it.

"Did he take Madiera by force?"

"No, but force isn't always so obvious, is it, Morgan?"

"No it isn't. Where does he have her?"

"At an old mission here in San Antonio. Presumably, he wanted her to see what he has planned. Perhaps to impress her to the point where she would show interest in him as a man."

"Are you afraid he'll succeed?" Morgan asked.

"On the contrary, I'm more concerned that I know he will fail. What he will do then? I don't know." Lopez got up. He straightened. "I treated you badly before. I do need your help. I do not understand men like Villa and I do not have men to stand against him."

"And you can't stop helping him?"

"Not now, not even with Madiera's return. He has

too much influence, too many followers among the people. I can only trust to God.''

"Well, mebbe we can give God a little hand," Morgan said. "Let me talk to him. Mebbe I can get some of the help I need. Villa can get closer to what he wants and we can get his mind off your daughter.''

"Hiee!" Lopez slapped his forehead. "I have forgotten, *señor* Morgan. A telegraph cable for you. It came just minutes before you walked in. I was angry. I intended to read it." He picked it up and handed it to Morgan. The gunman felt a knot in his stomach when he saw the point of origin. Uvalde!

> Morgan,
>   It's Marsh Coltrane. Kid put out the word
> and got took. Marsh left word he'd be con-
> tacting Charity. Word has it he's got 70 men
> riding for him. We got less than 30. Miss
> Charity is scared.
>
>   Jed

"Bad?" Lopez asked.

Morgan folded the telegraph cable and stuffed it into his shirt pocket. "It's not good," he said. "But first things first. I'm riding out to see Villa.''

"You'll need something from me. Something in writing. Without it, Villa's men will not let you pass.''

"Yeah," Morgan said, "write it out." He took it but he'd already decided not to use it unless it was forced on him. Over his signature, de Lopez wrote a clearance request. Then he penned out a small map giving Morgan directions to the old mission.

Mission *Concepcion* was located about a mile and a

half from the old Alamo mission. In many ways, it resembled the original Alamo complex where Texas freedom had found its first breath of life. Morgan made the last half mile on foot.

De Lopez had not underestimated Villa's security but he had underestimated Lee Morgan. Morgan gained the outside wall using a handy tree. Once inside, he found it easy to measure the pacing of the Mexican guards. Villa fought like a guerilla in the field but had been caught up with military procedure in the barracks.

Morgan made easy work of violating Villa's security ring. It was planned to protect him against the advent of a mass attack. One man, Villa believed, was no threat. The old mission chapel was now Villa's private quarters. They included a dining room and it was there Morgan found the Mexican bandit leader. He was relieved to find Villa dining with Madiera de Lopez. Two men stood guard. One at the door and another in the anteroom which served as a kitchen.

"Buenos noches, señor Villa," Morgan said, dropping through an arched window, gun drawn. It was leveled at Villa's head. The Mexican's eyes got big but then he picked up a napkin, wiped the drooping mustache, leaned back in the high-backed chair and laughed.

"Buenos noches, señor Morgan. Congratulacion y bienvenido." He laughed again. "You have done what a hundred men could not, *mi amigo.* Come—come, join us."

"I'd just as soon make it a little more private," Morgan said, motioning with his pistol toward the guards. Villa nodded and barked orders in Spanish. The two men, both prepared to die in defense of their leader, nodded and, thought Morgan, both looked relieved. A moment later, they were gone.

"Are you comfortable, *señorita* de Lopez?" Morgan asked. She smiled and looked at Villa. "I'm fine, thank you."

"Did you come to rescue the lady, *señor* Morgan?"

"Hardly," Morgan said, holstering his gun and pulling a heavy chair from beneath the table. He accepted the wine Villa offered. He sipped at it. "I came to deal."

"I understood a bargain had already been struck between yourself and the *señorita's* papa."

"It has—for hauling freight. I want a deal with you."

"And you sneak up on me with a *pistola*?" Villa shrugged but he was still smiling. Obviously, Morgan's entrance had impressed him but he was anything but frightened.

"I did that only to prove a point."

"My *vaqueros* would have killed you even if you had killed me. It is because they too fight for Mexico—not for Villa."

"Still," Morgan said, his voice more firm now, "you'd be—uh, *muerte.*" Morgan smiled and added, *"Mi amigo!"* Villa laughed. Morgan handed him de Lopez's note.

"Muy bueno, señor. Muy bueno! You could have *walked* it but you did not." Now, Morgan knew, Villa was properly impressed.

"What then," Villa began, sitting back and firing up an oversized Havana, "can a humble *vaquero* do for such a famous *Americano pistolero?*"

Morgan was being patronized. Indeed, Villa was aware of what could have happened had it been

Morgan's intent to kill him. But the young revolutionary would not yet be persuaded of much else.

"Have you heard about the raiders operating between here and the border?"

"*Si.*"

"I want your help to get rid of them."

"You want Villa to risk his life and the lives of his faithful followers to rid Texas of a few *culebras*?" Morgan frowned. "*Serpientes.*"

"Snakes," Madiera offered.

"Hardly," Morgan said. "They're a little more than a few snakes. They represent an anti-revolutionary faction in this country pitted against you and financed by your enemies in Mexico." If nothing else, Morgan now had Villa's attention. He sat up straight, scooted the chair toward the table, flicked the ashes from the Havana and then leaned into Morgan.

"If you speak the truth, *Yanqui*, then I have a lieutenant who must answer for his failure. If you lie," Villa said, "I will have you shot. I have heard of a *caudrilla* raiding small ranches to the south. Are these your anti-revolutionaries?"

"They are." Morgan noted that the revelation brought a puzzled look even to Madiera's face. "There's more to their raids than stealing a few cows or horses."

"Tell me, Morgan, tell me everything."

Morgan did. He concluded with, "Simply put, if the ranchers south of here are run out and Marshal Coltrane reclaims the Double C, you've got a severed supply line and some well trained guerillas operating between you and your base of supply."

Villa grinned. "You speak like an old *hombre*

ejercito.'' Morgan shook his head and shrugged. "An army man, *señor.''*

"Doesn't take an army man to figure this one. Just a few facts."

"I have a good man. *My lugarteniente.''*

"Your second in command?"

"Si.''

"Well, he missed something."

"He has never done so before."

"There's always a first, Villa."

"Shall we see?"

"Please, let's do." Morgan turned and saw the look of concern of Madiera's face. Morgan was pushing on Villa—and on his top man. Morgan smiled to reassure Madiera but inside, he was wondering if all the information he had was accurate enough to have gone this far this fast. One little lie would be all Villa needed. He was suspicious of almost everyone outside his immediate circle of power anyway. Morgan had heard a story or two of U.S. government agents trying to infiltrate his band. They had simply disappeared. If Morgan looked like anything to Villa at this point, it was probably another Yankee spy.

Pancho Villa had a much bigger reputation than he had a physique. He was about five feet, eight inches tall and a little overweight. He looked much more like a man who should have been lounging in some *cantina* with a *señorita* and a bottle of *tequila* than leading a revolution. This, Morgan found out a few minutes later, was most definitely *not* the case with Villa's *lugarteniente*—his first lieutenant.

The man was nearly six feet four inches and his frame appeared as solid as a brick wall. Morgan thought he'd weigh about 230 pounds. He was dressed immaculately but what Morgan saw first was the man's six-shot revolver. He wore it on a hand tooled, cross-strapped shoulder rig. The holster, black leather with hand-tooled silver decor, was firmly in place high up on the man's left chest.

When he responded to Villa's summons, he entered the room, obviously surprised to see Morgan. He smiled at Madiera, instantly noted the absence of the guards and then eyed his superior with concern. He and Villa then conversed, fast and in Mexican. They spoke in tones too low for even Madiera to hear. Finally, Villa returned to his chair and the other man took up a spot at the opposite end of the long table.

"*Señor* Morgan, I would like to introduce you to Juan Miguel Delgados." Morgan pushed his chair back, stood up, fully expecting to meet the man half way and shake hands. Instead, Villa spoke an addendum. "He tells me, *señor*, that you are a *mentiroso*. A—"

"A liar," Morgan said before Villa could translate.

"*Si, señor.*"

"Tell him for me that he's mistaken."

Villa sat down, poured himself some wine, leaned back and said, "Tell him yourself, Morgan. He was educated in your country." Villa laughed. He was playing Morgan on a string and now he'd brought the cat in to get in a few licks.

"If he speaks English," Morgan said, "then he's already been told."

"I know of this gang," Delgados said, "and I know of the man who leads it. He seeks to reclaim his own ranch and as much more land as he can. Perhaps, from what I have heard, he deserves to get it back with interest. But either way, *señor* Morgan, he has nothing to do with the revolution, Mexico or General Villa.'' Delgados smiled, stepped slightly to his left, away from the table and added, ''That makes you very stupid, *señor*, or a liar.'' Madiera de Lopez was suddenly feeling frightened. She stood up. She addressed herself to Pancho Villa. ''Hasn't *señor* Delgados overlooked the possibility of an honest mistake?''

Villa, enjoying the discomfort he was creating, just shrugged. ''Ask him, *señorita.*''

''I've asked *you, señor* Villa. I am *your* guest, not his, and I believe I am due the proper courtesy.''

''If the *señorita* expects the proper courtesy,'' Delgados said, sharply, ''then she should conduct herself in accordance with the dictates of proper upbringing. Perhaps you have lived too long on the wrong side of the border, *señorita.* In Mexico, a lady does not interfere in the affairs of men.''

''What men?'' Morgan said, scathingly, gesturing first at Villa and then at Delgados himself, ''an unshaven, overweight peasant boy and a fancy dan *vaquero* who happens to speak well.'' He'd gone all the way. He was in, Morgan thought, up to everyone's neck. The consolation, of course, lay in the fact that if he didn't pull it off, he wouldn't have to face anyone in failure. He'd be quite dead!

''Morgan!'' Madiera spoke the word. Villa was on his feet. Delgados moved, cat-like, to Madiera's side, grabbed her arm and pushed her into the chair.

''You put another hand on her,'' Morgan said, ''and I'll kill you.''

''You have already earned yourself the opportunity to try, *señor* Morgan, with your insult.''

"Then you did know you were being insulted. Good. That shows real progress."

"You go too far, *Yanqui,*" Villa shouted. Three doors opened and no less than three men appeared in each of them.

"Sure you've got enough men to back you, Villa, or are they here to back your fancy lieutenant there?"

"Out," Villa screamed, "get out!" Morgan had the Mexican bandit riled. Too, he could see the flush of anger on Delgado's face. "You have pushed Villa too hard."

Morgan suddenly backed up about eight steps. He did a half turn. Now he was positioned diagonally from both Mexicans.

"No, Villa, you pushed too hard and too far. I rode in here to show you you're not invulnerable and to deal honestly. I tried to remain pleasant and play your game for awhile. Game's over."

"I demand satisfaction," Delgados said. "Tomorrow morning in the courtyard."

"Bullshit! You've been reading too many dime novels, Delgados. You want me? It's here and now. You and your boss man." At last, an expression on someone's face which Morgan could recognize. Villa, who constantly wore crossed *bandoliers,* each supporting a pistol and a double holstered rig on his waist, stood, mouth agape, staring at Morgan's right hip. He had assumed the stance necessary for a gun fight. Morgan had made the last bet. Now it was Villa's turn. Morgan thought that Villa was very much aware that he would be the first to die. That Morgan would die too seemed little consolation when the chips were finally down.

"You have my honor," Delgados said. Morgan noted the tentative tone. He guessed Delgados would be fast—rattler fast. Morgan had already decided that if push came to shove, he'd take out Villa and pay the price.

"No, Delgados, I don't have the time. As to honor, by what I've seen and heard here tonight, the only one in the room deserving of any is sitting down."

"I've had enough, *señor,*" Pancho Villa said. He turned toward Delgados. "It is ended."

"I think not, General."

"It is ended. I wished only to determine the *Yanqui's* grit. I am satisfied."

"I am not."

"Delgados!"

"Tirar, yanqui!" Morgan did—faster perhaps than he had ever drawn his gun before, and he made a particularly exaggerated display of foolish bravado. He fired one shot a little high, blowing off the Mexican's silver-encrusted sombrero and fired a second shot right straight at the Mexican's right hand. The bullet struck the cylinder of the Mexican's gun, ripping the weapon from his hand and tearing into the flesh of his palm.

Morgan had been right. Juan Delgados, the tall, handsome and soldierly lieutenant to the would-be Mexican dictator, was fast. Lee Morgan had simply concentrated his entire being into emerging not only the victor but appearing invincible where gunplay was concerned. He knew he had the skill. Rarely did he have to use all of it in such a concentrated or showman-like form. He detested playing with guns. He'd seen a few young gunnies with their border shifts and Curly Bill spins. They were all dead. In this case, however, Morgan had determined that the situation was probably the exception which proved the rule.

The skill he displayed left Delgados wincing in pain, still blinking at the speed with which it all happened, and Pancho Villa open mouthed. The gunsmoke was still curling into the air. Again the doors had opened and gunmen stood, weapons pointed, waiting Villa's order. Lee Morgan eyed the Mexican bandit, reckoned that he was no longer in any danger from Villa and holstered his gun. Madiera de Lopez took a table napkin and began treating Delgados' wound.

9

Morgan's climactic display to Pancho Villa was simple. After initial treatment of Delgados' wound by Madiera de Lopez, Villa's own physician took over. Morgan informed villa that he would be with the de Lopez family for one more day if he, Villa, wanted to talk further. That done, Morgan took Madiera by the arm and the two of them walked away from Villa's compound.

At just after noon on the following day, Morgan was informed that Pancho Villa was waiting for him in de Lopez's library.

"Buenos dias—rayo pistolero," Villa said, smiling. It took Morgan a few seconds to translate. Villa had called him the lightning gunman."

"Señor Villa."

"I will make my point quickly, *señor*. I can do as you have requested, help you to eliminate the gang of raiders one of two ways. The first is an agreement with you, personally. The second would be forced upon me by the circumstances—the need. It would not include you, Morgan. I would prefer the first. A deal." Villa smiled now, removed a cigar from his pocket, eyed it, took out a second and offered it to Morgan. Morgan accepted.

Both men wet the ends of the Havanas, bit off the tips, found matches, lit up the cigars and puffed several times. All the while, they were making a concerted study of each other. Villa knew what Morgan wanted. Morgan knew that Villa wanted something in return.

"If you take out the raiders, Villa, I've got what I want. Why should I deal?"

"If you do not, I will simply offer up as many men as I have to for replacement of you. They will work free for the supply wagons. I will refuse to assist anyone so long as you are involved." Villa smiled. "You will not be popular, *señor* Morgan."

"On that alone," Morgan replied sharply, "I wouldn't be losing much. I'm none too popular anywhere in Texas right now anyhow."

"Then you do not wish to hear my offer?"

"Talk's cheap, Villa. Listening is even cheaper."

"When this is over, when the raiders are finished and the supplies are flowing into my citizens' army in Mexico, you will join me. You will find nine more like yourself, *Yanqui pistoleros,* and you will join me." He held up a finger. "For one year. You will report directly to me, but we will work together. You will be special, a guerilla force to hit and run."

"I don't sell my gun for that long to anyone," Morgan said. "Besides, Villa, your threat of getting me fired doesn't wash. If the raiders are eliminated, I've no reason to stay around. The Masters family hired me to ride shotgun because of the raids."

"There is one more thing," Villa said, standing up. "If you refuse me, I'll have you hunted down and killed." He puffed on the cigar. "I will spare no effort—use as many men as it takes for as long as it takes. But I will find you, and I will have you killed."

Morgan considered the young Mexican. He knew Villa meant what he said. Here was the case in point. Villa's abuse of what little power he already wielded. He'd let the *revolucion* go to hell, Morgan thought. Delay it for as long as it took. Use whatever resources, no matter how short the supply, just to prove his point—just to kill Morgan.

"Is there a word in Mexican for sonuvabitch!"

Villa laughed. "If you wish, Morgan, you may try *bastardo* on me. It has been more widely used."

"I get the pick of the men in your outfit to use against the raiders, and I lead them—alone."

Villa frowned. "Some will not like to follow you."

"You tell 'em they will or I'll kill 'em with your blessings."

"You push me again, Morgan," Villa said. This time there was only half a smile.

"Well," Morgan said, getting to his own feet, "there is one other little thing."

Villa laughed. When he stopped, he walked over and slapped Morgan on the shoulder. "*Mi amigo,* if I turn you down, you will kill me right here, right now."

"You may end up making a good *Presidente* after all, *señor* Villa."

The deal had been cut. Neither man even considered the possible double-cross of the other. They shook hands. Just before they separated, Morgan told Villa that the first man he wanted was Delgados. Delgados, Morgan said, could select the rest of the men. Villa concluded that he would never want a man like Morgan hunting him. Both men seemed able to anticipate the other. Villa had intended to insist that Delgados be included in the selection process. Villa had reasons which were different from Morgan's for the choice. But both men knew the other's. Delgados represented the missing, written contract.

Morgan sent a telegraph cable on the morning before he rode out of San Antonio to return to Uvalde. It asked for a meeting at the Double C for that evening. In the interest of a timely delivery, he sent it to Luke Masters.

Morgan reached the five mile perimeter around the Double C about sundown. He was surprised by the increased manpower on duty and had to talk for several minutes before convincing those who stopped him that he was Lee Morgan.

He was not greeted with smiling faces when he finally entered the study at the big ranch house. Lucy Masters reached him first.

"We have a traitor in our midst," she said. "One of Charity's men took our last wagon yesterday to pick up supplies for the ranch here. She has stopped using the company in Del Rio. He got hit half way back. She sent out five men to look for him early this morning." Lucy looked down and shook her head, fighting back tears. "They found him hung from a telegraph pole. The wagon and supplies were both gone."

"Charity?"

"She and some of the other women are with the man's wife. He'd been here for many years."

"And word about Jimmy Willow or a meeting with Marsh Coltrane?"

"No."

"Where's Jed?" Morgan asked, looking around the room. "With Charity?"

"A message came into the telegraph office about half an hour ago. They sent a boy out to get somebody to pick it up. Jed went. It may be word from Marsh."

"Yeah," Morgan said. He was still looking at the long faces. The enthusiasm to make a fight was waning fast. Even his news from San Antonio might not be enough to turn the tide if things kept going sour. "Got any coffee?" Lucy nodded. "Mind gettin' me a cup?" She went to the kitchen. Morgan went on in. One or two spoke to him with a bare greeting. Most just nodded.

Lucy brought the coffee and then disappeared again. A few minutes later, she returned, this time in company with Charity Coltrane.

"Morgan, we'd best talk to these folks. Some have already said they want to pull out before Marsh hits them direct. I don't know if we can hold 'em or not. Did you get—"

"I got more than I went for," Morgan said, "but I think we'd better wait for Jed. Whatever I say needs to be last, particularly if Jed's news isn't good." Charity nodded.

"Let's give Jed a few more minutes before we get to the meeting—" She wasn't yet finished when the front door opened. It was Jed Railsback.

"Marsh wants to meet Miss Charity up at the Willuh Bend line shack. Sunup day after tomorrow. She comes in alone."

"Exactly where is it located?" Morgan asked.

Charity anticipated him. She shook her head as she replied. "Not in a spot to do what you're thinkin' about. It's on a ridge overlooking what we call the Rimfire range. Man in that shack can see for twenty miles in every direction on a clear mornin'."

"You feel any different than you did?"

"No."

Morgan turned to the gathering. "You all heard. Now let me add something. I've got men—well arms, well led professionals. Between them and you men here who have followed Jed, we can put an end to Marsh Coltrane." Morgan looked now at the Willow clan. "And we'll get Jimmy back, but we have to have a little time. Charity Coltrane is a woman you all know. You know her courage. You know her word. She can buy us that time. Then we'll have to fight. Some will have to die. Anybody that wants out—go now. No hard feelings, no effort to change your mind, no questions asked. But if you go, do it now. We have to know where we stand and with who."

Jed, Morgan, Charity and Lucy stood together, eyes scanning the group. Men shifted in their chairs. Wives looked at their faces. Some looked toward the dining room where they knew the children were gathered. It was accounting time. The books would have to be opened to all. The debits and the credits weighed against one another. Finally, each man would have to look into his own soul, and each woman into her own heart.

"Me an' muh missus—we got a boy out there somewhere. We got a lot o' work put in. Some hard, lean years, an' a few good ones as the Lord saw fit to give 'em. We'll stay with you. Least 'til we find out who an' what we're up ag'in."

"Mister Willow here speaking just for himself," Morgan asked, grasping the single opportunity he might get to pump some courage into the gatherings collective veins.

"Nobody needs to talk up for me an' mine, I'm Thad Talbert and we'll stick. We'll fight if it makes sense to do it." He looked around the room and then back at the leaders. "Heard tales about you, Mr. Morgan. Some of 'em didn't make you out to be the kind o' man I'd care to ride with, but I'm not much on talk. Action gets the job done. You said you had men. Where are they?"

"San Antonio. They're Mexican revolutionaries. They're led by a man who started out about the same as you people in a tough, lawless land, but with a dictator who collared them all. The Masters Freight Company is going to haul supplies for these men. In turn they've agreed to help clean out the raiders. After all, the Masters been hit as hard as anybody."

"I got no quarrel with ridin' with men like that if'n the Masters don't. But I'll say one more thing. Whatever happens had best happen soon. Most o' the folks sittin' here can't stand many more losses."

It was Charity who spoke up now. "Then give me time for my meeting—two more days. That's all we ask. Just two more days."

"What about the law?"

"I don't think we can count too heavy on any help from the law. It's too thin and scatterred in these parts. Still, I'll do my best to bring in some assistance from the Rangers."

The meeting broke up. Charity wanted Morgan to stay the night again. She didn't get the opportunity to ask him but he would have turned her down in any event. Lucy Masters wanted to talk to him. So did Jed Railsback.

"You're full o' surprises, Morgan," Jed said. They were walking toward Morgan's horse. "Didn't know you had any special love for Texas Rangers. Or them for you."

"I didn't say that, Jed. I just said I'd try to get them to give some help. To do that, we've got to get their attention."

"Uh huhn—'bout how I had it figured." Morgan mounted up. Lucy had already headed her carriage back toward town. She was pulling out with several of the other families, but they'd soon split up. Morgan didn't want her on the trail alone. Jed nonetheless caught hold of the harness on Morgan's mount. "One more thing, Morgan," he said, looking, Morgan thought, worried. "Luke wasn't here tonight. You know why?"

"Sure, Jed. He was feeling poorly. Stayed in town. Planned to work out some schedules for freight runs into Mexico for de Lopez."

"He warn't in town, Morgan. Leastways he wasn't at the house or the office."

Morgan looked puzzled. In Uvalde, even whore houses and saloons were in short supply if a man was of such a mind. Luke Masters wasn't. He nodded at Jed and spurred his mount.

Morgan caught up with Lucy within a mile. She stopped while he tied his mount to the rear of the buggy and then climbed up beside her. They said nothing for a ways but it was Lucy who finally set the theme.

"Morgan, what are you feelings—uh—I mean your feelings as a man about Charity Coltrane?"

Morgan didn't think there were too many surprises left in this situation. Obviously there had been one. "Whatever they might be," he said, trying to conceal his surprise, "I'd think they'd be my affair." He turned and looked into Lucy's face. "Don't you?"

"Under other circumstances—yes."

"Under *any* circumstances, Lucy, my personal feelings are just that—mine. At least 'til I'm ready to share 'em."

"Did you bed her?"

Morgan snorted. "You don't quit, do you?"

"That's no answer."

"It's none of your damned business. Hell, that situation wouldn't even be all mine to tell. Would it?"

"She'll be riding out tomorrow. She'll have to leave tomorrow to get to the line shack by sunup the next day. She wanted you to stay with her tonight."

"You don't know what the hell you're talking about."

"She's in love with you, Morgan."

"Bullshit!"

"She said so."

"To who?"

"To no one. It's in her eyes when she looks at you and in her voice when she speaks." Lucy half smiled and then looked way, straight ahead. "Even the gentleness of her touch."

"More bullshit! Female intuition."

"Or male naivete."

Morgan studied Lucy. The conversation was too far from dead center at this point to really make sense. Maybe Lucy knew that he and Charity had bedded down and maybe she didn't. Either way, Morgan thought, the depth of this conversation was a cover for something else. What?

"Where was your dad tonight?"

"Home—why?"

"No he wasn't. He wasn't at the office either."
Lucy's head jerked to the left and she looked into
Morgan's face. She realized his revelation was no simple
ploy just to change the subject.

"Who told you that?"

Unlike Lucy, Morgan had an answer. He didn't
hesitate to use it. "Jed Railsback. When he went in for
the message, he stopped by."

"Why?"

"I thought maybe you could tell me. Why would Jed
go to see your dad? And having gone to see him, why
didn't he find him?"

"I—I don't know." Morgan considered her. He
believed her. She looked shocked and puzzled.

"Let's get back," Morgan said. Lucy nodded.
Morgan cracked the whip.

The cartage company's offices were locked and dark.
When Morgan and Lucy finally reached the house, Lucy
was scared. She hurried inside, shouting for her father.
There was no answer. She began a search—room by
room. Morgan joined her. Luke Masters was not there.
It was nearly two o'clock in the morning.

"They've taken him—like Jimmy Willow."

"I'm riding to the office." Morgan started for the
door. He turned back. "Get your coat back on. You're
going with me." Lucy looked at him and nodded.

Luke Masters appeared to be asleep. He had long
since moved a small cot into a back room, an old
storage area at the freight company's office. He was
stretched out on his back, arms folded across his chest,
feet crossed at the ankles. His boots were off. His eyes
were closed and he seemed to have a smile of satis-

faction on his lips. The only flaw in the scene was, at first, undetectable. Luke wasn't breathing!

"Back off, Lucy."

"He's—oh God—Daddy!" Lucy covered her face, stifled a scream, which, instead, came out in short, pitiful whines. Morgan then saw the wound. Left side of Luke's head, midway between his ear and his temple. A small-caliber weapon, probably a Deringer, had inflicted it. There were black smudges on the flesh—powder burns. At first glance it appeared Luke Masters was a victim of his own hand.

Morgan covered him up and had a quick look around. He led Lucy to the front office. He sat her down. She was staring into nothingness. He searched until he found a bottle of whiskey. It was nearly full so he took a long pull for himself and then poured a smaller quantity into a water glass for Lucy. She did not protest but neither did she consume it quickly. Morgan nursed it into her a little at a time.

"I'm taking you back to the Double C." What the whiskey hadn't done, his statement did.

"No you're not. I'll not set foot on the Double C again—ever!"

Morgan frowned. "Why? No one there did this to your father."

"The hell they didn't. If Charity Coltrane had given us her freight business from the beginning—we—Dad—there would have been money enough."

"You can't stay alone." She stood up. "It's only temporary." She walked to the big rolltop on the far wall. "Charity won't even be there after tomorrow. You said so yourself." She opened the top drawer. "I'll be out there most of the time too 'til we take to the fight with Marsh."

She reached in, extracted a short barreled Allen and Wheelock revolver and turned to face Morgan. Only then did he see the gun. She cocked it. Morgan dived. Lucy fired. Morgan rolled. Lucy fired. The shot blew out the coal oil lamp, shattering the shade and spreading burning oil onto nearby papers. Morgan grabbed her, spun her toward him and let go a solid punch to the jaw. Lucy dropped. Morgan doused the flames with the whiskey—all but one shot. He downed it and slumped into a chair.

Morgan was surprised to find Jed Railsback bedded down on the floor in the main house at the ranch. Jed was equally shocked at Morgan's appearance.

"I thought Miss Charity would be sleepin' better with me right here."

"Yeah, Jed. Good idea."

"What the hell brings you—"

"Luke Masters is dead. Shot through the head. Somebody tried to make it look like he did it himself."

"Goddam! Lucy?"

"Outside. Out cold. I had to hit her."

"I'll wake Miss Charity." Morgan nodded.

Morgan related the events, how he and Lucy returned to Uvalde while Charity prepared coffee. She had furnished a sleeping draught to Morgan and he'd gotten it down Lucy's throat. Jed sat nearby, keeping an eye on the young girl.

Charity took Jed a cup of coffee and then returned to the kitchen. She spiced up Morgan's coffee with some top grade Irish whiskey. "Luke Masters was no coward. I don't give a damn. Luke wouldn't do it."

Morgan looked up. "I told you what I found. Now let

me tell you what I didn't find—a gun. Who do you know that Luke knows—who also owns a Deringer?"

"I only know one person who owns a Deringer. Thirty-two caliber." Charity sipped her coffee, looking at the floor. Morgan didn't ask the obvious question. He gave her time. She took it. She looked up. "Me. My Daddy gave it to me when I turned eighteen."

"Where is it?"

"Upstairs in a drawer in my chiffonier."

"You sure."

"There has only been two people in my bedroom recently. The gun was there two days ago. You know who the people were."

"Get it, Charity."

She wasn't gone a minute. She smiled at Jed as she went through the living room. She noticed he was not in the chair when she returned. She was moving faster. The Deringer was gone.

"It's gone," she said. Morgan had both hands on the table. His eyes shifted to the corner of the kitchen. She turned her head to follow them.

"Sit down, ma'am."

"Jed!"

"This what you're lookin' fer?" He held up the Deringer. He did it with his left hand. His right hand was full of Colt. He had it leveled at Morgan's head. "Warn this gunman not to try pullin' on a drop—leastways not on mine."

"He's one of the best pistol shots in the county, Morgan."

"I've got nothing to lose," Morgan said to Charity and then turned back to face Jed and continued, "have I, Jed? You'll have to kill us both anyway."

"Nope. Just you Morgan. And not just yet."

"Jed! Jesus! *Why?* For God's sake! You've been with me for—with the Double C—"

"More years than I care to count, Miss Charity. An' now I'm about to git paid right for 'em."

"From Marshall Coltrane," she asked, scowling at him.

"He needed somebody on the inside. He made it worthwhile. You don't have to die, ma'am. I got that worked out with him."

"You bastard! You back-shooting, low life, lying bastard!"

"Easy, ma'am, I know you're riled. But don't crowd me too much."

Morgan sensed Jed Railsback's growing anger. He intervened. "Why Luke Masters?"

"Too bad 'bout Luke—wasn't figured—just happened. He caught me fakin' that message to Miss Charity."

"Faking the—you—there isn't any meeting with Marsh?"

"There's a meetin', ma'am—just not the way you figured it."

"When Jed? Where?"

"Here. Tomorrow. The rest o' the folks in the valley will figger blood's thicker'n water when it's all over. They'll hear how you sold out to your brother."

"And Morgan?"

"He gits turned into the Rangers in place o' Marshall. Them lookin' alike an' all. Well, it kind o' takes ever'body off'n the hot part o' the stove."

"Jed." The voice was soft. It shouldn't have been there. It was. Jed's head jerked. His eyes blinked at the black smoke and red-orange flame that belched out of the end of the six-gun right straight at him. The look he assumed was so firmly established in the final seconds of his life that it locked the muscles in place in the first few seconds of his death. He had no place to fall. The force of the heavy caliber shell shoved him against the wall. He hung there a moment and then slipped into a sitting position. His arm went limp and the pistol he was holding slipped from it. Then, his head dropped to the left.

Lucy Masters slowly lowered the gun to her side and then released it. It clattered to the floor. Charity was at her side. Morgan got to his feet, checked Jed and then stood up and turned.

"The message couldn't have come from Marsh," Lucy said. Both Morgan and Charity looked puzzled and at each other before turning back to Lucy. "I hauled the material up in that country to build that line shack at Willow Bend. Jed paid me to do it out of his own pocket. Told me never to say anything to you, Charity, but he needed it built fast and the outfit from Del Rio couldn't bring the lumber in time."

"My God! Marsh wouldn't have known about the Willow Bend shack. He'd been gone for years. I—I should have thought."

"Something bothered me about it when I heard Jed's words. I didn't know what it was 'til we got home. Then it hit me. Thing was, I couldn't be sure if it was you, Charity, or Jed or maybe both. I had to get out here to find out."

"Well I'll be a sonuvabitch," Morgan said. "You were playacting that whole time. Goddam! Sarah Bernhardt herself could take a lesson from you."

Lucy smiled. Charity hugged her. Lucy looked into Charity's face. "I'm glad it wasn't you."

"She's—she's slipping, Morgan," Charity said. Indeed, Lucy Masters had faked almost everything except the sleeping draught. That, she fought off as long as she could. Between the whiskey, Luke's death, Lucy's fears and the powder—she was gone. Morgan and Charity got her bedded down. Morgan moved Jed's body out of the kitchen. Charity calmed the hired help and Morgan told the men on duty that the shot had been accidental. The story would hold until later in the day—he hoped. Charity began cleaning up. The job was nasty. Morgan helped.

"What now?" she finally asked.

"What we've been waiting for. If Jed Railsback is the only turncoat on your spread, we've got an edge. If we use it right, it ought to be enough."

"You've got a plan?"

"Yeah, but it'll keep 'til daylight. We'd best try to get some sleep." Charity was too exhausted to protest even a little bit. She nodded. Morgan bedded down on the floor near Lucy. His handgun was nearby, cocked when he fell asleep.

10

Young Jimmy Willow was more than grateful for the hard biscuit, water and plate of red beans. His captors hadn't fed him since noon of the previous day. Too, he was glad just to see another face—even the face of Ike Larraby. He didn't see it long. Ike jammed the food through the window opening, eyed Jimmy with disdain and then slammed the wooden shutter down again and locked it. Just then, Cole Larraby shouted at his brother. "Marsh wants to see you, Ike. Right now."

"Shit," Ike mumbled to himself. He was hungry. He'd planned to eat. If he got orders from Marsh, he might not get the time to eat. He shrugged and trudged off toward the old shack Marsh Coltrane had commandeered for his private quarters.

Ike and Cole Larraby represented half of Marsh Coltrane's four top guns. The other half were Larraby cousins, Lafe and Tom Caspar. Of the dubious quartet, Ike was the most disgusting. He rarely bathed. Not even his brother would sleep in the same bunkhouse with him. His stringy, matted hair and never-trimmed beard

were both lice infested as was his crotch. He kept both
hands busy just scratching in one place or another.

Ike Larraby was also ugly. The left side of his face
dipped in toward his teeth. No hair grew along the
almost inch wide scar. The scar itself ran from the
corner of his mouth all the way to the base of his ear. It
had come to him in a knife fight when he was fifteen.
He won the fight, but there was no help for his face. The
bleeding had been stopped with gunpowder. The cheek
had been held together for weeks with bailing wire. The
flesh grew crooked, gapped and otherwise improperly.
Ike could barely stand the sight of himself. Others
turned away if he looked at them head-on. Mostly he
didn't. He talked out of the side of his mouth, face
turned away and head cocked. It only added to the
horror.

Along with his brother and their cousins, Ike Larraby
was one of the most vicious, useless and totally ruthless
human beings ever to sit a horse. The lot was wanted in
damned near every state south of the main line of the
Union Pacific. The crimes for which they were sought
were as varied as their twisted minds could create. Rape,
robbery, murder—downright butchery. Ike was the
worst.

The four of them, given almost total license to
practice their treachery by Marsh Coltrane, in turn kept
the rest of Coltrane's human dung heap in line. Any
complaints were handled by one of the four. Usually
with a six-gun. There were damned few complaints. If
nothing else could be said of them, the Larrabys and the
Caspars were deadly gunhands. Too, they had one more
common bond. Their numbers gave them a collective
backbone. Separately, the lot had none.

* * *

Ike found Marsh just finishing his breakfast and studying a hand drawn map which rider had brought in that morning, presumably from Jed Railsback.

Marsh took the last bite of his biscuit, mopped up egg yoke, jammed it into his mouth and followed the disgusting looking blob with a swallow of coffee. He sloshed the combination back and forth between his cheeks, swallowed, sucked his teeth and then looked up.

"Jesse brought me this map. Jed stole it from old man Masters." Ike grinned. "They plan to run a dozen freight wagons south out of Uvalde loaded with men. Figure to camp between Crystal City and Carrizo Springs. Figure we'll hit 'em there and get hurt bad."

"Where they runnin' the *real* thing?"

"Right straight into our laps," Marsh said. He motioned to Ike who joined him at the table. Marsh jammed his index finger onto the map. "Twenty-five wagons will leave Uvalde two full days ahead of the decoys. Follow the Neuces River north and then west toward Rimfire Range. Then they'll cut back south to Brackettville." Ike studied the map. Scratched at himself. Marsh winkled up his nose as Ike's body odor began to reach his nostrils.

"Jeezus howdy—them wagons'll be right out in the open when they start trailin' between Salmon peak and Turkey mountain," Ike said. Then he stepped back and looked his crooked look at Marsh. "So would our boys if'n that there's a trap."

"It's no trap. The trap is south. Hell! It's right here, Ike. Right from old man Masters himself."

"You sure are mighty trustin' o' Jed Railsback."

"Right now I am," Marsh said. "When it's over, Ike,

you kill him.''

"Sure Marsh—sure. Just don't forget what you promised me'n my kin for our troubles.''

"I won't, Ike. Don't worry. Charity and the Masters girl are yours. I don't want to see that bitch but once, when she comes to the line shack.''

"I still think that stinks. Somethin's rotten. What if she wants to deal?''

"Then we deal. Then you get her, Ike. And the girl.''

"An' what about the kid out there in the shack?''

"Soon as I show Charity he's still alive and hear what she has to say—you kill him too.''

"What now?''

"Take a half a dozen men and stay on that ridge behind the Willow Springs line shack 'til you see Jed and Charity coming. Make damn sure they're alone. Damn sure!''

"Yeah. Okay, Marsh, but I still think it stinks. They was s'posed to be there three days ago.''

"Stop thinking, Ike. I do the thinking in this outfit, not you. Charity Coltrane is no goddam idiot. She's got to play it safe too. I figured she'd want some proof that Jimmy Willow is alive. Besides, the delay gave me the chance to get Jed involved direct. She's got anything up her sleeve—Jed's right there to kill her.''

"Yeah. I guess.''

"You'd best get riding.''

"I'll send Lafe and Tom—'' Marsh Coltrane was pouring himself another cup of coffee. He stopped, whirled and scowled at Ike Larraby.

"Did I say send Lafe and Tom? I said *you* go, Ike— *you* personal. That means what I said. It don't mean Lafe and Tom.''

"I'm s'posed to be your ramrod. I'm your goddam top gun, Marsh. Not no fuckin' errand boy."

"You're what I tell you you are, Ike. Nothing more. You'd best remember that. I give you an order. I got a reason for it. You want what you've been promised. Then you do what I say when I say and how I say." Marsh turned completely now and faced the ugly gunman. "Unless you think you're good enough to run this whole show without me and good enough to take over. Is that what you think, Ike?"

Ike Larraby had often imagined himself in fine clothes, gambling at the best places in New Orleans or San Francisco. Things Marsh Coltrane had already done—briefly at least. Things he planned to do again. Sometimes, Ike fantasized about Charity Coltrane—naked—standing before him and forced to do his will. Other times, he saw her tied, spread-eagle to a big four-poster—helpless before him. Of all Ike Larraby's fantasies the one he most cherished however was drawing on Marsh Coltrane and beating him. Marsh had given Ike plenty of chances to try. Now he had another. Ike studied Marsh's face for a minute. Then he shook his head. The fantasy was still a fantasy. Ike was good. But he was scared to pull on Marsh Coltrane.

"Didn't mean nothin', Marsh. I'll ride out."

"Good. When you're sure about the situation. When you've talked to Jed himself, then you get word back here and I'll ride in."

"Yeah, Marsh. Okay."

"And one more thing, Ike. Make goddam sure Charity doesn't hear you talking to Jed or getting any ideas about Jed's loyalty. We lose him we get set back quite a spell. I set it up this way so they'd buy it. Don't fuck it up.''

Marsh's words grated on Ike Larraby. No other man could have spoken to Ike that way—not and lived. The fantasy flashed through his mind again. Then it was gone. Ike nodded.

Lee Morgan, Charity, Lucy and the others would have been much more at ease had they known Marsh Coltrane's lack of trust in any judgments not his own. The reason, of course, came from Marsh's trust, once before, of his father. The total self-reliance was the chink in Marshall Coltrane's armor. The fact of it was that Ike Larraby's suspicions were worthy of considerable attention. Jed Railsback had made the worst possible kind of mistake—the kind that proved fatal.

Jed had done so out of pure greed. Faking the message to Charity to lead her to the line shack was only to insure himself a firmer grip on control of his own destiny. He didn't completely trust Marsh, and he'd hoped to use Charity as a bargaining chip. Luke Masters accidentally stumbled into the situation, which then developed too fast for Jed's thinking processes. Jed's contribution to the events had now become considerable and all of it on Morgan's side of the ledger.

In the three days since Jed's death, Charity had faked her own message. She agreed to ride with Jed, to the Willow Springs line shack. Morgan, in rummaging through Jed's belongings, learned that the line shack had been the message center between Marsh and Jed. It was no doubt why Jed used it that last time, not thinking that Marsh wasn't supposed to know anything about that line shack. Lucy Masters, a little removed from the center of the problem and knowing her father would never have taken his own life, had caught Jed's error. The offense now shifted, albeit tenuously, into Lee Morgan's hands.

Marsh Coltrane had responded to Charity's request for the meeting and agreed that one man, Jed Railsback, could accompany her. Marsh still wanted to be certain but Lee Morgan was already certain. He pulled one of the ranch hands, a man about Jed's size and build, and planned for him to pose as Jed. Morgan knew there would be lookouts. Morgan himself would ride out ahead, secret himself in an appropriate observation position and wait. He'd trail whoever rode back to Marsh Coltrane. Then, he'd have a first hand look at the enemy camp.

The plan was so simple it somewhat frightened him. Often, Morgan knew that the easiest-looking situations were those which most quickly fell apart, as Jed Railsback's had. But, with the receipt of Marsh's message, so far so good. A phony map of Masters' first shipments for the Mexicans, information about the real route, and an offer from Charity should make for a careless Marsh Coltrane. Morgan had contacted de Lopez and Pancho Villa. A single word would move their men into position. Finally, Morgan had also sent a dispatch to Texas Ranger Headquarters. He hoped its contents would bring a few additional guns into the Double C camp.

"Good morning." Charity and Morgan were drinking coffee, for the most part in silence. Lucy had been staying at the Double C since the tragic events of three days earlier. This was the earliest she had risen during those days—and the best she'd look or sounded.

"Lucy," Charity said, smiling, "you look rested for a

change.''

"I feel it, for a change.'' Charity started to get up. "Please, let me. I've been little use lately.'' Charity nodded, understandingly. Lucy sat down, sipped her coffee. "I'm sorry about my outburst yesterday. Waiting on Dad's proper burial is only sensible.''

"Still hurtful,'' Morgan said. "But we can't afford to let Marsh Coltrane know what's happened.''

"I appreciate your letting them put Daddy in the ground next to your own father, Charity, even if it's just temporary. It would have been much, much harder just to see him stuck any old place.''

"We'll have a proper service when he's moved. A proper tribute to him too when this is all over.''

Lucy nodded. She closed her eyes and bit her lip, fighting back the urge to cry. "God! I wish it was over. How many will die before it is?''

"A damn sight fewer than before,'' Morgan said, "because of Luke Masters.''

"I hope so. God, how I hope so.'' Lucy sighed. "Well then, have you decided on the first freight run for de Lopez?''

"If *he's* ready, yes,'' Morgan answered. "Jim Keyes, the man who's posing for Jed, and I will ride out early in the morning. If Charity's meeting with Marsh goes well, and I'm able to find their main camp, the freight will start moving two days later. A day after that—''

"It should be over.''

"Yeah.''

"I'm still worried about you, Charity,'' Lucy said. "If someone spots Jim Keyes as a fake—''

"They won't,'' Morgan reassured her. "All he's

doing is dropping her at the line shack and riding back south to wait."

"You don't think any of Marsh's men will want to talk to Jed personally."

"I doubt it. Stupid of Marsh if he tried. He'd run the risk of Charity spotting it and knowing she's got a turncoat working for her. No. I'm betting against that."

"Alkali told me yesterday. He's got seven more teamsters hired. By tonight he should have enough men for the wagons going in both directions. Where do Villa's men join you?"

"Just outside Laguna. Once we're sure Marsh's men are in position, Villa will provide fifty men for the wagons and another fifty to move into Rimfire Range and hit Coltrane's bunch from the rear. Any and all who get out of that ambush and make it back to the base camp will find me and the ranchers waiting for them."

"And south?"

"You take the five wagons out of here. Alkali and the real shipment will pick you up at La Pryor." Morgan grinned. "You all ought to be down in the *cantina* at Piedras Negras by the time Marsh Coltrane discovers he's been scalawagged."

Lucy Masters got to her feet. "I've got to get back to town. There's plenty to do and—" she took a deep breath, swallowed and forced a smile, "it keeps me occupied."

"I'll ride with you," Charity said.

"No. I've got business in town anyhow," Morgan said. "You get yourself ready to ride out in the morning, Charity. I'll ride with Lucy." Charity nodded.

* * *

Lucy hesitated at the front door of the Masters house. She glanced at Morgan. He felt for her. He unlocked the door and they both went in.

"You okay?" he asked. She nodded. "Then I'm going to the bank and the mercantile before I ride back to the Double C. I'll look in on you before I leave town."

"I'll be at the office by then. Stop there."

Just shy of an hour later, Lucy Masters was about to unlock the front door at the Masters Cartage Company's office when she heard a shout. Half a block away, Lee Morgan was just leaving the bank. The shout had come from one of two men positioned in the middle of the street. Even at that distance, Lucy could figure the action.

"Texas Rangers, Coltrane. You're under arrest!"

"Dear God," Lucy mumbled. She grabbed the Winchester from its saddle sheath, levered a shell into the chamber, aimed the weapon down the street and fired. She levered a second shell into place and fired again.

The shots dug up the dirt in the street short of the two rangers. They did get the men's attention, however, and Morgan took advantage of the situation. He dived behind a water trough.

One of the rangers got off a shot as Morgan dived. He missed but Morgan knew he'd not get out without a fight. The second man, armed with shotgun, fired both barrels at the trough, tearing out most of the streetside wood. The water drained out and Morgan's haven of safety was cut down to the thickness of the trough's building side edge, about two inches. Morgan rolled, came up to his knees and fired. The ranger with the shotgun dropped—hit in the leg. Morgan twisted to face the other man. He heard Lucy scream. Then—the lights went out.

Morgan thought the room was turning when he first opened his eyes. It proved to be a pinata suspended from the ceiling and gently blown by an outside breeze. He sat up. He winced. He gently felt the back of his head. The knot was good sized.

"That's as far as I'd go if I was you, mister—unless you're tryin' for another goose egg—or worse."

Morgan's eyes focused. He looked toward the voice. He saw a big man. Two hundred and fifty pounds, he thought. He was sitting in a rickety chair, its back against the wall. An adobe wall. The man had a scatter gun, both hammers locked open, leveled at Morgan's chest.

"You've made one helluva mistake," Morgan said.

"Don't think so, Coltrane. Think it's you and your lady friend what did the mistake makin'. But it's over now."

Morgan thought: Lucy! Jeezus! She'd fired too. "Where's the girl?"

"Cared for."

"Goddam it! I'm not Marshall Coltrane. My name is Lee Morgan. I sent a telegraph cable to your office from the Double C ranch. I asked for help to get Coltrane."

"Shut up!"

"Look. I can prove I'm not Coltrane. Send a rider out to the Double C. Coltrane's sister is out there. She'll tell you who I am."

The big man stood up. His vest pulled back and Morgan saw the ranger's badge. The man moved toward Morgan menacingly. "I said shut up, mister. I meant it."

Morgan scooted back on the bed. Out—he'd be no use to anyone. A quarter of an hour passed. "Mind if I smoke?"

"You ain't got the makin's. Yo ain't got nothin', mister." Morgan was about to protest again when he heard a door—then footsteps. He looked up. The big man got to his feet. The door to the room opened. One of the two rangers who'd confronted him on the street stepped into the room.

"On your feet, Coltrane, and turn around."

"I'm not Coltrane," Morgan said, standing. The ranger moved over and let go a meaty fist into Morgan's belly. The gunman, caught off guard, grunted and half doubled up. The ranger grabbed a handful of hair, twisted, turned Morgan around, jerked his arms behind him and secured his wrists in handcuffs.

Morgan recognized nothing. Once outside, he knew why. The old adobe was abandoned and nowhere near town. In fact, as Morgan was helped up on a horse—not his own—he scanned the countryside. He could not recognize any of it. Not even along the horizon. He thought: How the hell long was I out? Where did they bring me? Where to now? And where the hell is Lucy?

There were three men. The big one led Morgan's horse. By his own reckoning, they were moving south. He had to do something. What? Half an hour later, Morgan did recognize his surroundings. They were riding into La Pryor—some twenty miles south of Uvalde.

In front of the Zavala county courthouse, Morgan saw his horse and Lucy's. On the second floor of the courthouse, Morgan was taken into an office which had no sign on the door. A man was pouring himself a cup of coffee when they walked in. He had his back to them, sitting down behind an old desk. He turned and looked up.

"Hello, Coltrane." Morgan eyed the man. He remembered where he'd seen the face before. The San Antonio newspaper. This was Jute Yokley, District Deputy of the Texas Rangers. One mean sonuvabitch. Charity had told Morgan that it was rumored that Marsh had killed a man named Britt Yokley. It had happened in a whorehouse in El Paso. Thing was— young Yokley had a daddy who was—a Texas Ranger!

"I'm not Coltrane."

The man ignored Morgan. "Take his cuffs off and leave us be."

"Sir—he—"

"Do it!"

When they were alone, Jute Yokley sat down on the edge of his desk. He smiled at Morgan. "Do me a favor, Coltrane. Make a try for the window." The ranger took his gun from its holster and placed it on the desk. "Go for the gun, Coltrane. Please. Try me. Do me and Texas a big favor. You'll save the price of a hangin'."

"Goddammit, Yokley. My name is Lee Morgan. I look a little like Marsh Coltrane. But I'm not. Christ! The woman with me can tell you. So can Coltrane's sister at the Double C ranch. So can—"

Yokley back-handed Morgan. The force of the blow and the surprise sent Morgan back against the chair, nearly tipping it over.

"You cowardly, lying scum. I got two dozen people who'll witness to who you are." The big ranger grinned.

Morgan's arms were tense and his face twisted into a look of pure hatred. It was exactly what Yokley wanted. "Yeah, Coltrane. Get riled. Get *real* riled. Then I'll have an excuse to kill you." Morgan knew the man wanted one. Even a flimsy one.

"The woman. Lucy Masters. She's got nothing to do with any of this. Let her be."

"I'll take care o' the woman, Coltrane. Your worryin' days over somebody else are all over. Only one you got to worry about is you." The man stood up. He appeared as though he was going to turn around. Suddenly, he spun back and hit Morgan again—twice. Then he picked up the gun. He cocked it and placed the barrel on the bridge of Morgan's nose. "No one would know. No one would ever find out. What's saving you, Coltrane, is my desire to see you sweat and then hang."

After several seconds, the man eased the gun's hammer back down, withdrew the pistol and backed around the desk. "I'll tell you the fuckin' truth, Coltrane, I wasn't real sure I could keep from killin' you when I finally saw you. Now I want to see you at the end of a rope. But don't make any mistakes. You so much as breathe wrong and I'll kill you, Coltrane, a little at a time."

Morgan knew there was no point in continuing to deny his identity. Under no circumstances was this man going to believe him. He'd only make his situation worse and, he thought, perhaps Lucy's as well. He was also acutely aware of something else. They had refused to tell him Lucy's whereabouts. Now he knew why. As long as he didn't know where she was he wouldn't dare make a move, unless he didn't care about her. That, he thought, could be his salvation.

"You're holding all the cards," Morgan said. "What now?"

"We wait." The ranger smiled. "Don't want you to be lonely so we'll bring you some more company." Morgan frowned. "Billy!" The door opened. "Take him down with the girl. Cuff them together."

Morgan was led outside to the rear of the court building. There, he was taken into a storm cellar. A single candle burned at the bottom of the steep ladder leading into the musty room. Lucy sat huddled in a corner. Morgan saw her and considered his options. They were slim to none. He had a gun in his back and two rangers between him and freedom which, at best, might have lasted two minutes. A few moments later, he and Lucy stared at each other in the semi-darkness—handcuffed together.

"Are you all right? Did they hurt you?"

"I'm—" Lucy stopped. She looked into Morgan's face.

"What is it?"

"How would Jed Railsback have known that Charity owned a Deringer? How would he have known where she kept it? Why, my dad caught Jed by accident. Would Jed have even had the damned gun with him?"

"Jesus H. Christ," Morgan said. "Charity? It can't be! She was at the ranch the whole time."

"No she wasn't, Morgan. She left to be with the other women who were trying to give some comfort to her hired hand's wife." Morgan's brow wrinkled as he remembered. She wasn't there when he arrived. She'd been gone sometime already and she didn't come back for sometime after he arrived. She had time to go to town.

"All right, Lucy, I'll give it a maybe. You got a why?"

"She rode in to kill Jed. Dad got in the way. Jed was scared. He tried to find Dad. You told me so yourself. He even asked you about Dad. He didn't know about that back room."

"Charity did?"

"Yes. She was in it not long ago—with me."

"Lucy. Some of it makes sense, but it's pretty goddam thin in spots."

"Charity went upstairs that night for just a minute—or so it seemed. I was—well groggy—half asleep."

"Yeah. I sent her up there to look for that Deringer. It wasn't there." Morgan snapped his fingers. "Jed had it, Lucy. How'd he get it?"

"That's what I'm recollecting now. When she came back down, Jed—he—he got up. I remember them standing near the door to the kitchen. Then, Jed walked into the kitchen and Charity just stood there for a minute."

"To make it look good. Sonuvabitch! And she let *you* do what *she* rode to town to do—kill Jed Railsback."

The door to the storm cellar opened. The big ranger came down and hauled Morgan and Lucy to their feet. He took off the cuffs and stayed behind as they climbed back up the ladder. Once again, they were taken inside the courthouse and back to the second floor office. Charity Coltrane stood in the corner of the room. Jute Yokley pointed to Morgan.

"Is that man your brother?"

"Yes sir," she said.

"And the woman?"

"Lucy Masters. The one who stole the Deringer out

of my bedroom.''

"And used it to kill her own father to protect this—this filth.''

"Yes, sir. She killed my top wrangler too, Jed Railsback.''

"And this gunman. Lee Morgan. S'posed to look like your brother here. You know anything about him?''

"Only that this woman hired him. Got him killed so the law would be off of Marsh's trail. I think he was killed up in San Antonio.''

"Well," Yokley said, "I think I've heard all I need to hear." He turned, smiling at Charity, and said, "I never believed I'd see a woman with so little regard for human life and so much greed for land and power." He brought up his pistol. "But you're worse than any man I've ever come up against. You're under arrest, Miss Coltrane. We'll start with murder." Charity's jaw dropped. She looked, disbelieving, at Morgan and then at Lucy. Lucy was equally shocked. Morgan stood up.

"If we're going to keep that appointment with the real Marsh Coltrane, we'll have to ride now.''

"Morgan—I—'' Morgan smiled, helped Lucy up and put his finger to his lips.

"I'll explain it all on the way back to Uvalde. But you were doing a pretty good job down in that storm cellar of figuring out a few things.''

"You're a dead man, Morgan," Charity screamed. Two rangers pinned her arms and forced her into a chair. Morgan and Lucy could hear her sobbing as they departed the court house. Jute Yokley caught up with them outside.

"I'll have fifteen men, the best in Texas, up there in that camp on schedule.''

"We'll need 'em," Morgan said.

Morgan tied the horses to the back of Charity's buggy. She wouldn't be needing it. She was staying. The couple had gone near five miles before Lucy finally spoke.

"You've known all along, haven't you?"

"Not hardly. It came in pieces. Most of 'em you know."

"What don't I know," Lucy asked, smiling and then looking at Morgan and adding, "besides who you really are?"

"I'm Lee Morgan. On special assignment to the Texas Rangers for an old friend."

"That man Yokley?" Morgan nodded. "Did he pick you because of your friendship or because you resemble Marsh Coltrane?"

"Both. The first I owed him. He saved my hide once. The second came in handy."

"How could you be sure of getting the job with our freight line?"

"Couldn't be positive," Morgan replied, "but your dad got a little extra pushing that you didn't know about—from Jute."

"Dad—God—I—I still can't believe he's—" Morgan took Lucy's hand and squeezed hard.

"I wish to hell I could have stopped that. Everybody tried to warn your dad to back off. He was just too much a man to take their advice."

"Too damned stubborn is what Daddy was. He always was." Lucy looked up. "Today. I don't understand today. The treatment. The cellar. All that. Charity wasn't around."

"The second job for me in this little shindig is putting

the Coltrane clan out of business. The first was helping to find one Texas Ranger gone bad. Ends up he went bad by going to work for Marsh Coltrane.''

"It's all so confusing. It's almost too much for me."

"It was damn near too much for me. Helluv it is—it's not over yet."

"Just who was that bad ranger?"

"The big fella with the shotgun. Remember the little detour he took comin' down from Uvalde?"

Lucy's eyes got big. "You weren't unconscious that whole trip."

"Not hardly."

"Sarah Bernhardt might do well to take a lesson from you." Suddenly Lucy frowned and looked up at Morgan. "I was bait!"

Morgan didn't respond but he raised his pant leg, reached down in his boot and extracted Charity's Deringer.

"Damn you," she said. Morgan shrugged. "Well. What now? No Charity to ride to the line shack." Morgan didn't respond. Neither did he look at her. It didn't take her long to figure it out this time. "God! Bait again?"

"Got anybody else we can send?"

"And who goes as Jed?"

"That we don't change. But you two will never reach the line shack. I'll be there by midnight with half a case of dynamite. When you're close, I'll blow it. You two fire a few shots toward the ridge. You know, make it look like you think you've been set up."

"Then?"

"Then turn around and ride like hell out of there. I'll trail whoever back to the camp." Morgan looked down at Lucy and smiled. "And that's the other change."

Lucy looked quizzical. "What?"

"The wagons will move into the area tomorrow afternoon intead of the following morning. Villa has already been notified. I'll get word to the ranchers this afternoon instead of the following morning. Villa has

"Marsh won't really have time to find out what went wrong."

"Exactly. He'll have to move on the information he last got. It'll be wrong, but by the time he finds it out, it'll also be too damned late."

"God. How I wish it was over."

"Soon," Morgan said.

"You know, I still can't figure Charity. I mean—she already had the ranch and she hated—I mean I thought she hated Marsh."

"She did, Lucy. Still does. The ranch was small stakes. Charity was the contact on the American side of the border for the anti-revolutionary faction in Mexico. She stood to get damned rich if she could knock out de Lopez and Pancho Villa."

"But I thought Marsh was being financed by the Mexican government?"

Morgan smiled and shook his head. "He was and is! Charity was their insurance. Or competition. They don't give a damn who survives, just so long as somebody stops Villa."

"My God! It's all too complicated for me."

"Yeah," Morgan said, wistfully. "In my dad's day, everything was pretty simple. He always knew who he had to face. Not anymore. I guess it'll get worse as civilization makes more demands of itself."

"I don't think I want to be around in another fifty or

seventy five years,'' Lucy said.

"No. Me either. Too goddamn many changes already.''

Lucy smiled. She leaned up and kissed Morgan's cheek. He turned, surprised. She kissed him on the lips—gently. He felt a surge of heat in his groin. "Some things haven't changed,'' she said. It was a promise of things to come—literally! Morgan thought. That's one hell of an incentive to stay alive.

The buggy topped the crest of a hill. Before them, silhouetted against the gathering darkness, lay Uvalde.

11

The day matured, losing its newborn pink and taking on a bright, healthy, youthful appearance. It was just past seven o'clock and already warm enough to rouse the botflies. The horses on the ridge swished their tails to keep the pests in flight. There were five mounts. Among them Ike and Cole Larraby's.

The brothers sat atop a flat rock. Ike surveyed the sky with his crooked gaze. "Gonna be a hot sumbitch today." Cole said nothing. Instead, he elbowed his brother in the ribs. Ike looked perturbed but Cole was pointing. There were two black dots on the horizon. They slowly grew bigger.

Cole Larraby grinned, exposing short, dingy teeth. "Our booty?" He licked his scaly lips.

"More'n likely," Ike said.

Cole screwed his face into a scowl. "Goddam Marsh better not four-flush on this deal."

"He won't. He even tries," Ike said, fingering his pistol, "an' I'll kill 'em."

"So when, Ike? When do we git 'er?"

"Soon, little brother. Real soon now."

The black dots had grown to the size of riders. Ike stood up and walked back to the other three men. All of them were stretched out, hats over their eyes, trying to make up for lost sleep. He kicked at their boots and they sat up, mumbling collectively.

"We got company. Soon as I ride down an' make sure, you git ready to hightail it back to camp."

"How we gonna know it's okay?"

" 'Cause I won't be shot," Ike said, kicking the man who asked the question. "Dumb sumbitch."

"Ike!" It was Cole. "They're 'bout half a mile from the shack."

"You boys mount up," Ike said, and then he walked back to where his brother stood. Above and behind these men was another rider. Lee Morgan had seen the two black dots. He also could see the trail the five riders would have to take down to the ridge. He could drop in behind them anytime. He now looked farther away. He saw nothing, but he felt certain that somewhere out there, Pancho Villa and his men, young Luke Barkley and the ranchers and Jute Yokley and the Rangers were either riding in or were ready and waiting.

Morgan unsnapped a long leather rifle scabbard. He slipped the weapon out primed and loaded it. It was an old model, .50 caliber Sharps. The famed Buffalo gun. It was accurate to a fault and had the range he needed. He tested windage. He dropped to one knee, firmed up his elbow on a flat rock, shifted the rifle's butt until it was tight but comfortable against his shoulder. He sighted.

Morgan's target was a pony keg of water at the northeast corner of the line shack. Just above it, inside the shack on a shelf was the dynamite. He eyed the riders.

They were close enough.

The roar of the Sharps would have continued echoing for several more seconds had it not been drowned out by the explosion. The shack was transformed into a ball of red-orange flame, a belch of black smoke and a shower of kindling wood in a matter of seconds.

Immediately after he fired, Morgan put the rifle aside, reached into his shirt pocket and extracted a small mirror. He stood up, positioned himself and sent two flashes in the direction of the riders. It was the pre-arranged signal to let Lucy and Jim Keyes, the Double C ranch hand, know the position of Coltrane's men. A moment later, both were firing Winchesters toward the ridge. Morgan smiled with satisfaction.

Below him, Ike couldn't believe his eyes. "Shit! We been bushwhacked." The rifle shots toward them a few moments later brought another reaction—this one from brother Cole.

"They think we did it." Both men bolted for their horses. The other riders had already mounted up—sure of an ambush. Cole shouted, "Marsh ain't gonna be too fuckin' happy about this." He spurred his mount and got a good fifteen foot lead on his heavyweight brother. In his last observation on the ridge, Cole Larraby had been right on the money.

"You goddam yellowbacks," Marsh shouted. Only Ike and Cole had to answer for the hasty retreat. "You don't know who did what. You don't know if there were fifty riders on the other side of the ridge. You don't goddam know if you got trailed comin' here."

"Marsh. Shit! I thought we better hightail it back here."

"You thought! That's your goddam trouble, Ike. Always has been. You think. Jeezus! You fuck better than you think, and from what I've heard, you ain't worth much at that."

Ike's face turned from pale to bright red. His cheeks puffed up. He began to swell like a puff adder. "Ain't no sumbitch alive kin talk me down that way." He backed up.

"Ike! goddam! don't!" Cole stepped to his left and did a half turn. Ike's gun was already out. Marsh Coltrane had already fired. Cole took the slug in the side. At that distance, it ripped through his innards like a hot poker, ripping away everything in its path. Cole's mouth was, almost instantly, filled with blood. He choked, staggered and fell face forward. Ike just stared down. He didn't see Marsh's gun barrel tip up. Marsh shot Ike Larraby right between the eyes.

"Get these bastards out of here," Marsh hollered after he pushed Ike's body aside and opened the door. Suddenly their kinship with the Larrabys seemed quite distant to Lafe and Tom Caspar. They did Marsh's bidding. Finished, the Caspar boys reported to Marsh.

"You take half the boys and you make a raid on the Double C. Don't try to take it. Hit. Ride. Hit again. Kill every son-of-a-bitch you can see. If you can get as far as the house—do it. Burn everything you can reach. Raise hell!"

"We run into more'n we kin handle, Marsh, then what?"

"Ride straight for Uvalde!"

"Uvalde?"

Marsh Coltrane smiled. "I'll be there with what's left of the town and the rest of the men." The Caspars looked at each other and grinned.

Lee Morgan's plans, at least as far as he had been able to verify them, had gone off like clockwork. Timing, movement, even the mechanical things which sometimes fail men—jammed guns, wet explosives—all of it had worked this morning. Nowhere, however, could one man completely anticipate the actions or reactions of another. War presents this scenario in epic proportions. The field troops are but extensions of the will of the generals. The generals exert that will almost solely on what they believe their enemy will do in a given set of circumstances. Victory goes to the best guesser.

If Lee Morgan had guessed wrong, it was only because he didn't really know his adversary. He had underestimated Marshall Coltrane's obsession with vengeance. Caution and common sense were discarded along with immediate and long-term goals. Marsh Coltrane had been scalawagged. He didn't even care to find out by whom. Anyone in his path was fair game. Such madness defied Morgan's cool-headed logic, and completely scrapped his well oiled plan of entrapment.

Morgan did catch up with Lucy and Jim Keyes. Neither of them looked very happy.

"A Texas Ranger just left us," Keyes said. "They won't have their men up to Coltrane's camp."

"What? Damn! Why not?"

"Morgan," Lucy said, her voice almost trembling, "Charity escaped."

"Jesus H. Christ! How?"

"She—she's a woman," Lucy said, weakly. Morgan's mind flashed to Charity's bedroom at the Double C ranch. Her body—warm, naked and smelling of perfumed talcum powder.

"Yeah. Helluva weapon."

"Jute Yokley's got ever' man available to him lookin' for her."

"She'll likely head into Mexico. That's where she's got her contacts."

"What do we do, Morgan?"

"You two get back to the ranch. Hold the ranchers from moving out yet. Damn! Hold up the wagons too. I've got to get to Villa. Hopefully this won't do anymore than delay things a little. Fifteen men shouldn't stop us, but everybody's got to know." Morgan waited until Lucy and Howie were out of sight, then he turned back north. He hadn't ridden more than half a mile when he saw the dust cloud. He reined up. He frowned. He thought: It's either one helluva big buffalo herd or—

The riders came into view. He didn't remember ever seeing just exactly that kind of sight. Eight to ten abreast and, he reckoned, five to eight deep. At least fifty men. Maybe more. They were riding hell bent for leather straight for the Double C Ranch.

He turned, spurred his horse hard, and leaned into the saddle. He wouldn't be more than five minutes ahead of them. He'd have to trust Villa's own sense and good luck. The ranchers, the wagons and their teamsters, maybe even the ranch itself would be out of luck if these men got that far. Somewhere between them and the Double C they'd have to make a fight of it.

Marshall Coltrane's anger remained almost as dangerous for other men as it had for the Larraby boys. There was one exception. In his frenzy, Marsh forgot about Jimmy Willow. Locked up and shoeless, Jimmy had no guards. In their own haste to do their leader's bidding, none of the other men thought about Jimmy either.

Less than an hour after the deaths of the Larraby boys, the raiders' camp was virtually abandoned. Marsh, riding at the head of more than forty men, cut east over a hogback ridge and then due south on a beeline toward Uvalde. Jimmy Willow heard the commotion. He waited until he could hear it no longer. Then, he set about to free himself. He had done so in less than twenty minutes. He was startled at what he found—nothing. Nothing but two horses. The Larrabys didn't need them anymore.

Morgan, as hard and fast as he was riding, saw no signs of Lucy and Howie again. He did reach the five mile perimeter at the Double C. He had a decision to make and damned little time to make it. He scribbled out a note, affixed it to his black snake whip, removed all weapons and ammunition from his mount, slapped her on the thighs and headed her for the barn.

Morgan took up a position in a stand of trees. He hastily assembled what rounds he had for the Sharps—five of them. Loaded his pistol's sixth chamber, opened the last box of .44-.40 rifle ammunition for his Winchester and waited. He didn't have long to wait.

The first rider to die was a man next to Lafe Caspar. The Sharps round hit him in the chest and took him from his horse as though he'd been jerked from it by an unseen arm. The proximity of the riders was such that his sudden death was more a disruption than a catastrophe. Many of the second line rides reined up. Their actions resulted in similar reactions just behind them. Half a dozen men out ahead of the man who was shot didn't realize what had happened. The lot offered a skilled rifleman an inviting target and an almost stationary one.

Morgan hefted the repeater and began firing. The fusillade was devastating. Although it wasn't Morgan's intent, he hit several horses. The animals were rearing. Down they went with riders unable to dismount in time to avoid going down with them. Where no horses intervened, Morgan's deadly fire struck human targets. He killed eight men and three animals with the first twelve rounds. He shifted his position and targeted in on the first line of riders who were now aware that something was wrong. Three went down. None dead but all with wounds which would take them out of the fight.

The Caspar boys escaped Morgan's hail of fire but were forced to dismount in order to do so. They scrambled for the dubious safety of a shallow creek bed. Soon, they were joined by half a dozen of their fellow riders. None had yet seen their attacker or the direction of his fire.

Morgan shifted position again, managing to jam a round into the Sharps and completely reloading the Winchester. He singled out another target and dropped him with the Buffalo gun. It served to create as much fear among the living as it did death where it struck. Quickly, he brought the Winchester to bear again. By now, targets were becoming sparse. Nonetheless, he dropped five more men. Again, he shifted positions. This time moving south, toward the ranch. He did so amid a hail of bullets.

Almost as suddenly as Morgan had started the exchange, it ended. There was a pall of smoke amid the trees and into the open range land beyond. Morgan could no longer distinguish a clear target. Neither could his enemies.

"We best git the hell out o' here," Lafe Caspar said. His speech was a little muffled. The result of his pressing his face against the ground. "Marsh said we was s'posed to ride to Uvalde. Shit! We'll never git by here." Tom Caspar was trying to see behind him—without exposing himself. What he saw spelled big trouble. Half a dozen, perhaps as many as eight or nine men, had managed to round up their mounts—or someone's. They were getting out!

"We're losin' the boys. The goddamn yellow-bellies are skedaddlin'."

"I'll tell you fer a fact, Tom, that's what we ought do. We been hornswaggled."

"Shit, brother! Marsh'll kill us. Same as he did Ike an' Cole."

"I ain't goddam talkin' 'bout goin' back. Let's make Mexico." Tom Caspar eyed his brother. Both heard more horses behind them, men shouting to calm the animals. There were isolated shots now and again. Men firing at whatever they believed they saw. Albeit unknowingly, Lee Morgan got a vote in the Caspar's decision making process. His vote made it two against one for getting the hell out!

Morgan climbed a good sized willow tree, wedged himself into a fork in the trunk and found he could see the tops of a few heads. The Winchester removed four of them. The remaining rounds convinced the doubting Thomases. More than two thirds of the remaining riders simply panicked. Scrambling from whatever little shelter they had found, they crouched, ran, rolled or crawled back north out of range of the deadly hail of fire. First among them were Tom and Lafe Caspar.

Morgan climbed down from his perch, cast a parting glance at the disruption he'd caused, smiled and turned to head back to the ranch. He'd gone only a few hundred yards when a line of riders appeared. They were all carrying rifles at the ready, but moving cautiously. Howie Benton was at their head.

"Sounded like a damn war out here," Howie said, eyeing Morgan and looked puzzled.

"Coltrane's men. Or part of them anyhow. I turned them back. At least for the time being."

"Damn! Let's go boys. We'll finish 'em."

"Hold up, Howie," Morgan said. "We can't afford any losses. They're routed. Get every hand you can. Dig in." Morgan eyed the terrain in the direction from which the riders had just come. He pointed. "Back there. Just beyond the clearing. If they should regroup and try coming through here, you'll be in a good spot to hold 'em." Howie looked back. He also looked disappointed. He shrugged. Morgan climbed up behind him and the Double C hands rode back toward the ranch.

When Morgan reached the house, on Howie's horse, he found his own mount neatly tethered. He hurried inside, barely nodding at the two men who stood guard at the door. He was somewhat surprised to see them.

"Morgan! My God! I didn't know what to expect." Lucy Masters hugged the gunman—almost reflexively.

"Guards," he said, questioningly and gesturing with

his head toward the door.

"Howie insisted. So did Mr. Willow. I guess because of Charity."

"Yeah. Good thinking. Now you stay put. Part of Coltrane's outfit is out of action. For now at least. I've got Howie and the rest of the men about two miles out. Ready. I've got to reach Villa."

"Morgan," she swallowed. "Be careful."

Juan Miguel Delgados met his death well. No one could know how many of his enemies gave their own lives to assure the loss of his. But four at least died from wounds inflicted by Delgados' rapier.

Pancho Villa's favored *lugarteniente* was riding at the very forefront of his column. They were a dozen of Villa's best. Each a crack marksman and a veteran of almost all of Villa's earliest confrontations with *El Presidente's Federales.*

Delgados had taken these elite troops out ahead of his main column. It was one of two such columns being furnished by Villa. The young revolutionary zealot led the second column personally.

Delgados' column, by the simple process of rotten luck, cut Marsh Coltrane's trail thirty seconds before Coltrane's hell riders roared over the hillcrest. An uninformed observer would have most certainly reported that Delgados had ridden into a premeditated and well planned trap.

Both leaders and the men they led were, at the outset, shocked by the sight of the other. Coltrane's force, by weight of numbers and sheer momentum, had the advantage. That fact aside, the Mexicans inflicted serious damage to Marsh's riders and, more important, to his plan. Less a plan, really, than raw anger. Marsh realized that the Mexican riders could only represent the tip of a very dangerous iceberg.

Gathering his disrupted riders together again, along with more rational thinking processes, Marsh Coltrane ordered his men back down the ridge. There, he took stock of his remaining resources. Wiley Jenks was now Marsh's second in command, next to the Caspar boys. While Marsh paced nervously, Jenks took inventory.

"Five too bad hit to ride," Jenks reported. "Eight dead. Best I can figure, six run off."

"Fuckin' cowardly bastards!" Marsh's personal force, the men who were to have raided Uvalde, had lost almost half their number.

"Marsh, we can't." Jenks' courage floundered. "Mebbe we better figger—you know, somethin' else."

"Take two men," Marsh said, seemingly ignoring Jenks' words, "get back up on that ridge. Ride it north. Find the rest of those goddam Mexicans. I got to know what I'm up against. Send somebody south, down to the Double C. Get the Caspars back up to camp. That's where I'll take the rest of the men. Get there as soon as you can, but find me those goddam Mexicans!" Jenks nodded. He pulled two men from the ranks and was out of sight in a matter of seconds.

"Mister Coltrane. Mister Coltrane." Marsh whirled. A rider was coming in fast from the south. Several of the men nearby got to their feet. They recognized him as one of the men who'd ridden to attack the Double C. He reined up sudden and jumped from his horse. It was young Billy Eustis.

"What the hell are you doin' here?" Marsh asked, harshly.

"We got waylayed," he said. "Lost most o' the boys. Some jist run off. Lafe an' Tom too, I think."

Marsh drew his gun, raised it to forehead level and pulled the trigger. The nearby men, hard and tough as they were, recoiled in a combination of terror and anger. Almost all of them liked young Billy and he had displayed an almost puppy dog's loyalty to Marsh Coltrane.

"Mount up! We ride for camp." Twenty-four men mounted up. Those too bad hit to ride were abandoned —by Marsh's last order. He had begun his day with forty-three at his side. Fifty more had ridden with the Caspars. Marsh didn't see the seven who slowly dropped behind, slipped away and hightailed it for parts unknown. He knew only that any chance still remaining to him was valid only if he reached the fortification of the camp over looking Rimfire range.

Wiley Jenks did just as he was ordered. He found the rest of the Mexican force which Marsh Coltrane knew was out there somewhere. Jenks and the two men with him all went to the happy hunting grounds with the knowledge that they had successfully carried out their last mission in life. The Mexicans made short work of them.

Pancho Villa squatted down by his big, black stallion. He poked in the dirt with a stick. He rolled a stone about. He dropped his *sombrero* back from his head, letting it dangle by the chin strap. He waited. He got his report. Delgados had been ambushed. Villa stood.

"The *yanqui pistolero* dies." He swung into the saddle. "We ride, *mi amigos*," he shouted, waving his arm as he turned his horse. "*Sur!*"

South!

Jimmy Willow had sense enough to stay out of the open. He'd followed the base of the rocky ridge ever since he rode out of Coltrane's camp. Now, he watched the riders gallop by him, less than a quarter of a mile away, headed back to the camp and far fewer in number. After they passed him, he spurred Ike Larraby's chestnut mare and headed for the Double C.

Above him, headed in the opposite direction, on a deadly trail toward Pancho Villa's anger, rode Lee Morgan. He reached the break in the hogback. It levelled off and sloped downward.

Morgan started down.

"*Yanqui!*" The word echoed against the rocks. Morgan reined up. He looked. Villa was standing in his stirrups, his right arm held high. He'd halted his army. Morgan waved. Villa's arm dropped, crossed in front of him and drew his pistol. He drew the other one as well. He dropped the mount's reins.

"Villa!" Morgan shouted. The Mexican bandit spurred his horse, raising the pistols in front of him. Morgan thought: The sonuvabitch is a helluva horseman. The distance was about two hundred yards and closing fast. "Shit!" Morgan would have to gamble. He dismounted, slapped the horse on the rump, reached up and unbuckled his gunbelt. He raised it above his head. Villa had halved the distance. The Mexican leaned forward slightly, gripping the pistols tighter and beginning to steady them. Morgan waggled the gunbelt back and forth and then whirled it over his head for two full circles, turning loose as it began a third.

At fifty yards, Pancho Villa fired two shots. Lee Morgan went down. Villa reined up, the black stallion rearing and Villa displaying superb ability as he kept to the saddle and holstered his guns. He brought the animal under control. It snorted. Villa high stepped the big horse up the slope. Morgan got to his feet. His left hand was clamped over his right arm. His sleeve was dark with a wetness that seeped into the material from the hole in his arm.

"You think I will not kill you, *señor*, because you beg like a dog?"

"Kill me, Villa. Or be man enough to listen."

"More of your lies. Delgados is dead. A dozen of my best *vaqueros* are dead. I have seen no wagons. No guns except those turned against me. Tell me, *yanqui*, why should Villa listen?"

"Because Villa is wrong about *why* it happened. So either listen or kill me. No one but you and I will know you shot down an unarmed man."

Villa's cross draw was a blur of speed. The pistol landed at Morgan's feet. "Pick it up. I will give you that chance. If you do not, then you die a coward—not unarmed."

"Fuck you," Morgan said. He turned his back on Villa. The angry Mexican leader nudged the stallion, ramming into Morgan's back. Morgan went down, face first, hard. Villa dismounted, picked up his gun, walked to Morgan, grabbed Morgan's arm, rolled him over and Morgan cut loose with a left. Villa reeled and landed on his back. Morgan dropped to his knees, grabbed the pistol, cocked it and leveled it at Villa's head.

"You do not frighten me, *yanqui*. My destiny is not to die in this fight. I have much to do in *Mehico*."

"Well that's real interesting, *mi amigo*," Morgan replied, sarcastically. "Because my destiny is not to die here either. See. I placed mine with yours for a year."

Morgan smiled, "In *Mehico!*"

"*Caramba!*" Villa pushed up to his elbows. "If I defy destiny, *señor,*" Villa shrugged, "who knows what would happen to my country?"

"Yeah." Morgan winced. His arm hurt like hell. "Who knows?"

"Then, Morgan, tell me your lies."

Morgan tossed the pistol to the big Mexican and sat down, hard. "To hell with you, Villa. Get me back to the ranch. I'll tell you there. *That* is my *destiny.*"

12

A full-fledged *fiesta* would have been premature. The job wasn't finished. Still, there was ample cause to be thankful. Jimmy Willow's safe return headlined the affair. The information he carried with him proved a good secondary excuse for comsumption of tequila. He'd overheard much of what Coltrane's men had been saying before they rode out. The anger of Marsh Coltrane—planned destruction of the Double C ranch and the sacking of Uvalde. So much for revenge.

Marsh's failure had been most costly to Villa, even though Marsh's rag-tag army had suffered the highest losses. The dozen Mexican *vaqueros* had been worth any twenty-five of Marsh Coltrane's saloon dregs. Lee Morgan felt much responsibility for that—his misjudgement of Marsh. So much for the best laid plans of men.

Now however, the ledger sheets again on balance, there was a respite. Villa, no less angry but directing it toward Marsh Coltrane, posted twenty men in Uvalde. Another twenty were designated to remain at the Double C. Even with his reduced force and the losses of men who rode with Delgados, Villa could still field forty veterans. At dawn, the supply wagons would leave the ranch. Bait again. If Coltrane was drawn out, Villa would be waiting. If not, he and Morgan would do it the hard way.

Morgan's wound had ripped flesh and some muscle. No bone. Cleaned and bandaged, it would heal without lingering problems. For now, he had to avoid any need for his fast draw.

The ranch was quiet now. He could hear only the occasional squeal of a *señorita*. Villa had dipped into the till and brought forth some of Uvalde's finest for his men. Morgan chuckled at Villa's attitude. Morgan had asked him what *señor* de Lopez would think of such expenditures. Villa said: "The wages of sin, *mi amigo,* are always collected at inconvenient times and unexpected places."

"Morgan." The gunman's eyes were closed. His brow wrinkled. The dream seemed real. "Morgan!" The voice was louder but still retained its softness. He blinked awake. The doorknob turned. The gun came from beneath the pillow.

Morgan sighed. "Lucy. Shout. Knock hard. Bust right in. But for God's sake, and your own, don't sneak." Morgan sat up and put his gun on the nightstand. He wasn't wearing a shirt. Lucy closed the door. "Not here," he said, suddenly realizing the purpose of her visit, "not now."

Lucy slipped from the dressing gown. The body was young, firm, unexplored. The breasts jutted upwards at their peaks and the nipples were unusually large, more flat than round on top and stood erect. The shadows played across the flesh as Lucy moved. A dark patch caught a glimmer of light, then lost it and appeared again, mysterious and inviting. The thighs were creamy, the stomach taut, the odor irresistible.

Lucy approached the bed, dropped to her knees and pulled back the top sheet. She began kissing Morgan. His wounded arm first. Then she moved it above his head and kissed his chest. She worked lower. Morgan's thumbs hooked inside the bottoms of his underdrawers and slipped them down, raising his knees only long enough to remove the drawers completely. He stretched his legs out, spreading them slightly.

Lucy's fingers began drawing nothing on his bare flesh. Her lips and then her tongue became the center of her activity. Morgan's shaft hardened and crept up to meet her advances. She slipped the knob against soft lips, bit down ever so gently and flicked her tongue, lizard like, over this most sensitive area. Morgan groaned. His legs stiffened. Lucy lowered her head and began a rhythmic series of movements which alternated between her lips, tongue and teeth.

After several minutes, Lucy's hand slipped between Morgan's legs and she fingered, stroked and tickled the flesh. The combined sensations quickly brought Morgan to the verge of release. She stopped. She stood up. Morgan's breath was coming in short, rapid gasps. She gingerly crawled over him, tugging at him to turn to face her. He did. His sudden arousal lapsed into remission as he began administering doses of passion to Lucy.

She found it difficult to remain motionless but Morgan applied more strength each time she moved until, finally, she could barely move at all. The sensations were heightened and she moaned. He worked over her breasts, concentrating on those rigid and sensitive knobs. His hands and fingers explored further down. He spread flesh and found her clitoris. It was miniscule, but it must have been all nerve endings. Lucy convulsed and climaxed immediately. He stopped. She grabbed his hands and returned them to their former positions. He resumed his ministrations.

"Take me, Morgan. My God. Take me. Make me a woman. A whole woman." He did. They reached fruition of their efforts together, bodies writhing in physical pleasure which exceeded individual pain.

Morgan's wound came open. It bled. Lucy gently washed and rebandaged it. They lay, side by side in the darkness—the quiet, the depths of their own thoughts.

"It was beautiful," Lucy said. "More than I ever imagined." She touched Morgan's arm. "Was it good for you?"

"Very good."

"As good as Charity?"

"Better," he lied. "It was selfless."

"No it wasn't. It was for me. I wanted it. I didn't care how."

"You cared." Lucy accepted what he said. What she thought was one thing but why tarnish the dream.

Marsh Coltrane had finally come to his senses. He posted men along the ridge. He charged them with staying alert at risk of their lives if they did not. He had twenty-two men who would ride with him. Two more had skulked away in the dark of the night. He sat with Wiley Jenks.

"Yesterday's events may not be as tragic as they appear. Those freight wagons are to move today. By now those people must think I'm history."

"Mebbe, but how can we be sure them wagons won't be another trap?"

"Sitting here, we can't be sure," Marsh replied. "But I intend to be sure."

Wiley frowned. "How?"

"You're riding out, Wiley. You're the only man left in this outfit I can trust. With that kid running off, we don't know anything for sure. But you're not known hereabouts. Not by anybody."

"Damn risky. An' it's my neck."

"Half our men will be moving out at sunup along the ridge, out of sight. You parallel them. If they're sending wagons out, they'll start 'em at first light. If you haven't seen any signs by an hour after sunup, join the men and come back here. There won't be any wagons, leastways not comin' in this direction."

"And if I do?"

"Approach them." Marsh grinned and reached into his shirt pocket. "I borrowed this off a marshal awhile ago. Figured it might come in hand. Pin it on."

Wiley Jenks looked at the shiny tin star.

U.S. Marshal
Texas

Jenks grinned. He liked the idea. Mostly he liked the badge.

Barely a dozen miles away, two other men were meeting.

"You risk much that is not yours to risk, *mi amigo.*" Morgan had just informed Pancho Villa that a dozen wagons carrying the real supplies for his base in Mexico would depart the Double C at sunup, going north.

"It's mine," Morgan shot back. "I'm hired to shotgun the load and deliver it. You want it now?"

Villa looked puzzled. "No," he said.

"Then it's mine 'til I make delivery."

"If you fail, Villa will kill you without the talk this time, *señor.*"

"If I fail, somebody else will have beat you to it. Now you just make sure you're in position. If Coltrane's riders are still up there and the bait draws them into that range, you'll have one chance to end it."

"And Coltrane is mine, *señor,* personally."

"I've bargained away all I'm bargaining with you, *mi amigo.* Marshall Coltrane belongs to the fella who's man enough to get him." Villa shrugged and grinned, pointing at Morgan's arm. "Perhaps it would not be so wise for you to catch up with him. I hear he is very fast."

"Can you beat him?"

"Si *señor.*"

"And I can beat you. Wound and all. Should be about right." Morgan grinned. Villa did not. He was touchy about his gun skills. In fact, the young zealot wondered if he really could beat Lee Morgan. Wound and all.

"Adios amigo. 'Til we meet in *Mehico.*"

"See you, Villa," Morgan said. He turned. Villa galloped off. His men stirred up the dust as they trailed him. Morgan looked at the sky. A faint pink was bleeding up over the horizon. By daylight, Villa would be ready. He would give the Mexican half an hour. Then the wagons would follow.

He found no sign of Lucy when he entered the ranch.

He thought her still asleep. He went to the kitchen. The Chinese had prepared coffee. He poured a cup. He heard someone behind him. He turned.

"Jeezus!" Lucy stood in the doorway. She was clad in buckskins and had a Colt's .45 Peacemaker strapped on. "Who in hell do you think you are? Calamity goddam Jane?"

"Lucy Masters," came the crisp reply, "freight line owner and teamster. At least on this trip."

"The hell you are."

"Last night means nothing to me, Morgan. When it comes to business, you work for me. Remember?"

"And you stay in the office and do the bookwork."

"Uh uhn. If this load doesn't make it, there'll be no books. No office for that matter. I ride lead wagon or nothing moves out of here."

"Lucy. You're being a damned fool. What do you plan to do with that cannon on your hip?" Lucy drew, whirled, fired three times and took the wooden knobs off the corners of a cherrywood table. She breached the weapon and reloaded.

"I'll be damned!" Morgan shook his head. He couldn't help but smile. "Okay, girl, I'm convinced." He stepped over to her, leaned down, took her in his arms and kissed her. When she pulled back, Morgan said, "Just keep that pretty little head down. That's all."

She grinned. "That isn't the part I'd have thought you wanted me to protect."

"Isn't that the part that says *yes?*" Lucy laughed.

"Mornin' ma'am." Lucy halted the team. The man looked saddle weary, unkempt, and she was on her guard. So was her shotgun rider.

"G'mornin'," she replied. He eyed the line of wagons. Fifteen in all. She felt reasonably secure since there had been no signs of anyone for miles. In this particular stretch, the land undulated in gentle hills. A lone rider could be out of sight until he was almost on top of you. That had been the case. Larger numbers were easier to spot. Still, she wished Morgan was here. He was leading the second half of Villa's men and some of the ranchers whose preference it had been to see direct action.

"Heap o' freight you're haulin'. Where you bound?" Lucy noted that even as the man spoke, he was eyeing the depth of the wheel tracks.

"Del Rio," she said.

He frowned. "Little north o' the trail, aren't you?"

"Been a lot of raids lately. You must be new to the territory or you'd have known that."

"I'm new," he said, pulling back his coat and exposing the tin star. "Marshal Loving. Bert Loving. I'm down from the panhandle. Amarillo way. Man huntin'."

"I know most about. Who you runnin'?"

"Fella name o' Lathum. Charlie Lathum. Held up a stage."

"Never heard of him. But there's a lot o' ranches around where he could hire on."

"Well I'll snoop around a bit," the man said, tipping his hat. "Hope you have a good trip." Lucy nodded and snapped the reins."

"Hyah. Git up now. Hyah!"

"What do you think, ma'am?"

"I think," Lucy said, smiling, "Marsh Coltrane is

going to take the bait." She turned and looked at Willy Vestal, her shotgun rider. "Bert Loving was a deputy marshal up to San Angelo. Got killed a few months back."

"I'll be damned."

"Be alert," Lucy cautioned.

Up on the hogback, Lee Morgan, with the help of Charity Coltrane's eyeglass, had witnessed the meeting. Now, he watched the lone rider double back on his own trail, hugging the rocks along the ridge and riding hard toward Rimfire range.

"Yeah," Morgan said, "tell Coltrane he's got sitting ducks."

Wiley Jenks was back at the compound within an hour. By then, the heavily loaded wagons had only moved about five miles. Jenks downed a shot of whiskey and hurried to Marsh Coltrane's shack.

"Well," Marsh said, looking up. Jenks was smiling.

"Fifteen wagons. Deep ruts. Heavy loads. Woman. Spit of girl actual. Skinnin' the first one. Masters Cartage company it read. Out o' Uvalde."

"No escort riders?"

"Not a soul in sight. Two men to a wagon. Teamster an' a shotgun."

"That's thirty men right there."

"But they'll be in the open."

"Any of those wagons covered?"

"Nope. Not a damned one. No room in 'em fer any men. Looks to me like the real thing, Marsh. Sure."

"All right, Wiley. Good job. Now you get three or four men and scout the hogback. Stay on the sunup side. You see anything—anything at all that looks funny, you get on back—fast."

"How far south?"

"Just to the open range. If we hit those wagons—that's where we've got to do it. If anybody's laying for us—that's where *they'd* hit."

"How you goin' to do it—if'n you do it?"

"I'll take a dozen men, skirt the hogback to the south and come up behind 'em. You'll be drawing their fire. I don't want those wagons burned. If they're loaded with the real thing, they'll be ours, Wiley, and the contents will bring a pretty penny in Mexico."

"I'll ride out right now, Marsh."

"And when you come back, if everything is clear, take the men that will be left here and hit the wagons. I'm leaving now to get into position behind them. Any trouble at all—you or me—we get back here. That happens—tonight we'll split up and head for Mexico."

Pancho Villa sat beneath a willow tree by a clear, cool stream. He was puffing on a big Havana. His men lounged about in the buffalo grass, five of them posted to guard duty. He was three miles north and a mile back to the west of where Wiley Jenks would be looking. He was ready. He hoped Lee Morgan was as careful.

"Mendarez," Morgan said, pointing north and east along the ridge, "see there, where the hogback bows out to the west?"

"*Si.*"

"You take all but one man down along the ridge and into that bend. It's a box canyon. Post a man on top." Morgan pulled out his mirror. "When he tells you he's seen the flash—you ride right back here."

"*Si, señor* Morgan. I know of the canyon." Mendarez smiled. "I used it two days ago."

"Hell. For *what?*"

"To hide the *ametralladora.*"

"The—*what?*"

"How you say—*rat-tat—grande pistolero.* Canon. The gun of many bullets . . ."

"Good God! A Gatling gun?"

Mendarez grinned and shook his head. "*Si, si. Gatalino. Si!*"

"Mendarez. For Chrissake! Villa never said a word. Not a goddam word. That gun would make short work of this little war."

"It is for the *revolucion.*" Mendarez's face shed its grin and assumed a serious expression as he spoke, almost with reverence, about the *revolucion.*

"Shit! The gun won't do anybody any good if it doesn't get to Mexico, my friend. And it won't unless we use it here first."

Mendarez sighed. "It will take time, *señor.* She is *pesado.*"

"Pes—uh—yeah—heavy. Take along some help. But get that Gatling gun up here." Morgan watched Mendarez ride off. He still couldn't believe that Villa would have kept quiet about such a distinct advantage. "A goddam Gatling gun," Morgan mumbled, "and he never said a word!"

13

Wiley Jenks and ten men, riding about fifty yards apart, hell bent and firing pistols, charged toward the wagons. Jenks had ordered the men to close to a distance just out of pistol range, dismount and begin their attack in earnest with rifles. The cavalry-style charge was merely a ploy to draw the wagons' occupants' attentions. If everything was on schedule, Marsh Coltrane and the rest of the men would hit the freighters from the opposite side, unseen and unheard until it was too late. Thing was—everything wasn't on schedule.

Atop his observation point on the ridge, Lee Morgan had heard gunfire, a lot of it, a full five minutes before Jenks' men rode into view. Looking in the other direction, north, Morgan spewed a string of epithets when he saw no sign of Mendarez, the Gatling gun, and worse, no Pancho Villa. He looked back down at the engagement unfolding on Rimfire range. Coltrane's men were already at a standstill. Lucy knew the attack was coming and there were thirty men on those wagons. They would have no trouble holding off the attackers. They could not finish them however, and Morgan had no idea what had developed elsewhere. If Morgan was confused and in doubt . . . Marshall Coltrane was in shock.

As he'd planned, leading the remaining half of his men he'd worked along the ridge to the south of the open range and readied himself to attack the freighters from behind. He suddenly found himself under attack. Even more confounding to him, amid the dust and din of the gunfire, it appeared that whoever was attacking him were themselves being attacked! Marsh Coltrane, at that moment, probably enjoyed the biggest advantage of anyone in the field. He knew his dream was at an end, and he had no other reason to stay. He shot two of his own men to assure himself both a clear escape route and a horse on which to do it.

The Mexican named Mendarez found himself also confused, but more than that, scared as hell. Pancho Villa had made him personally responsible for the care and safekeeping of the precious Gatling gun. He knew his ill-tempered leader would simply have him shot when the truth was learned. Mendarez reached the box canyon to find the Gatling gun gone!

The extent of confusion and shock which stretched across the length and breadth of Rimfire range on that morning was not limited to just those men. One other man, as much angry as confused, and one woman were also players in the midst of the puzzling events. In part, they were responsible for some of them.

Charity Coltrane had, as Morgan guessed and the Texas Rangers assumed, fled into Mexico. There, using her feminine wiles and what facts she had amassed, Charity convinced Captain Luis Huerrera to lead a contingent of *Federales* into Texas and ambush Pancho Villa. Villa, she told the captain, would be totally vulnerable. Assisting *Yanqui* ranchers who were poorly armed and poorly led. Too, she assured him, he would receive unsolicited aid from Marshall Coltrane.

Charity had her facts straight. She just didn't have all of them. One of the most important, one which the good Captain would have liked to have known as well, was the loyalty of one of his lieutenants, and the man's real name. It was Francisco de Lopez! A matter of hours following Captain Huerrera's revelation of his plan to ride with Charity, young de Lopez left camp. He met with his sister, Madiera. In turn, the word reached the one man who, on this morning of mass confusion, was the one man who suffered not. Pancho Villa!

The peasant-turned-revolutionary had pulled men up from their hiding places in Mexico. They were his reserve units. Villa amassed them at a predetermined location and prepared himself with the Gatling gun to destroy Marsh Coltrane, Charity Coltrane and the northern Mexico contingent of government *Federales* in one fell swoop.

"*Prostituta! Ramera! Hija de la Diablo!*" Captain Luis Huerrera spewed the verbal venom at Charity Coltrane as Villa's hordes poured down upon the hapless *Federales* from two directions and the Gatling gun laid down a withering and fatal fusillade from a nearby ridge. Huerrara shouted the words, "Whore. Bitch. Daughter of the devil," as he reached for his handgun. Charity drew one of her Colts and shot him through the head.

At the beginning of the attack, Huerrera watched

with satisfaction as his men massacred the small band of riders who had followed Marsh Coltrane. Charity, mounted on a black stallion and attired in Mexican riding clothes, smiled at the captain, sensuously.

Certain of victory, the praise and an elevation in rank from *El Presidente,* and Charity Coltrane's favors, Huerrera was a happy man. Minutes later, his dream turned into a fatal nightmare.

Charity galloped from the field, headed for the one haven of safety closest to her. Her beloved Double C ranch. There, in a hidden wall safe, she had more than ten thousand dollars. Her dreams too had been shattered, but not her life. She would find a new one, deep in South America.

Lee Morgan was about to ride down to the wagons, flanking Coltrane's men, when more than fifty of Villa's men poured the hogback ridge to the north. Almost at the same time, Mendarez returned smiling.

"It is *acabado, señor. Terminado*—uh—"

"Over," Morgan said, frowning, "finished!"

"*Si.*" Morgan still wasn't happy. But he listened. Mendarez told him what had happened. One of Villa's lieutenants had caught Mendarez between the box canyon and the ridge.

"The sonuvabitch could have let me in on it."

"*El Generale* tells no one of such a thing. No one."

"Well he'll by God tell me from now on, or he's got no lightning-fast *Yanqui* guns."

Less than ten of Marsh Coltrane's hired guns lived to fall into Villa's hands. Nearly half of the Mexican *Federales* surrendered. Ultimately, they would transfer their loyalties to Villa. Most government soldiers were but *peons* themselves, forced into government servitude.

Morgan had just finished telling Lucy Masters of the turn of events when Villa himself rode up. He dismounted, smiled, shrugged and said, *"Siento hacer esto. Perdonar mi amigos?"*

"Shit! You're sorry. Goddam, Villa. Do you realize the risks you took?"

"Nostros area de guerra. Hay mucho. Grande riesgo."

"Goddam it, Villa, speak English. And don't give me that crap about being at war and great risks. We're not at war," Morgan said, gesturing toward Lucy, "and from now on, she gets full protection from your men or no goddam freight leaves for Mexico. At least not on any wagons run by the Masters Cartage Co." Morgan got to his feet. "You understand me, *señor* Villa?"

Lee Morgan was mad. Damned mad. Villa walked back to his horse, opened the saddlebag on one side, removed a thick envelope and brought it back. He eyed both Morgan and Lucy and then handed it to her. She glanced at Morgan and then opened it. Her thumb flipped the edges of the bills. Money. American money. More than Lucy Masters had ever seen all at one time.

"Twenty-five thousand American dollars, *señorita,"* Villa said. "That much again when these wagons reach my fortress in the hills of Mexico. From that money, you hire men, pay them as you choose. The rest, *señorita,* is yours."

"Gracias," Lucy said. Morgan frowned. Lucy scowled back to him.

"Shit," Morgan mumbled.

"Muchos gracias," Lucy said.

Mendarez rode up. He looked anxious. He dismounted and hurried to Villa. He reported in Spanish. Much too fast for Morgan to translate. Villa shook his head, frowned and then turned to Lucy and Morgan.

"The woman was not among the *Federales*. Captain Huerrera's body was found among the dead. But *señorita* Coltrane was not killed or captured."

"Marshall Coltrane?"

"No, Morgan. Both, at least one of my men report, both escaped the field and rode south."

"Together?"

"No, but perhaps to the same destination?"

Lucy looked at Morgan. "The ranch?"

"Yeah."

"I'm going with you."

"Not this trip," Morgan said.

"Damn you! Stop giving me orders." Morgan's right arm moved like lightning again—wound and all. He snatched Lucy's gun from its holster. "Keep her with this train, Villa. Head for Mexico."

Villa smiled. "You ride out to face *yanqui banditos* skilled with guns and ready to kill because they are cornered, and leave me with a wildcat." Morgan couldn't help but grin.

Charity killed two of her own ranch hands coldly with deliberation and skill. Inside the house she killed her long-faithful Chinese cook. She pulled a carpetbag from a closet, hurried to the wall safe, opened it and smiled with satisfaction when she saw the money. She quickly placed it in the bag. It was then she heard the squeal of a floor board behind her. She stood and whirled around.

"Hello, little sister." Marsh had not followed

Charity. Indeed, he had not seen her on the battlefield. Pure chance and memory had dictated Marsh Coltrane's actions. He knew that there was always a sizeable cash fund secreted somewhere at the Double C.

"I'd hoped you would have been one of the first to go," Charity said. Her tone was laced with poisonous contempt. Marsh was eyeing the twin forty-fives. He smiled. Then he looked at the carpetbag and glanced down at the open safe.

"I'll relieve you of that, little sister."

"Like hell you will. I killed to get it. You think I won't kill to keep it?"

"If you were good enough. Probably. But you're not facing two men who trusted you. I saw their bodies when I rode in. And," Marsh said, "I'm not an unarmed Chinaman."

"You bastard!" Marsh grabbed the door, pulled it and jumped back into the hallway at the same time. Charity fired two shots. They were close but neither struck home. Marsh would have killed her outright but for one thing. His gun was empty!

Charity jerked the door open, fully expecting Marsh to run down the hall or try for the stairs. He was just outside, back pressed to the wall to Charity's right. The move he made caught her totally by surprise. He knocked her cold. He grabbed the carpetbag, checked its contents and then removed one of her Colts.

"Rest in peace, little sister."

"Coltrane!" Marsh turned. He fired. Morgan fired back, his bullet ripping through the carpetbag. Marsh made for the back bedroom. It led onto a roof top from which he could drop to the ground. Morgan took the stairs three at a time. He paused for only a second to glance down at Charity. He heard the window open. He ran. Marsh was already on the roof. He looked through the window, saw Morgan and fired. Morgan was forced behind the door. Marsh Coltrane dropped to the ground. Luck still riding with him. Charity's black stallion was tethered at the hitching rail. She had come through the kitchen.

Marsh heard a voice from behind him. Another of the hands. He whirled and pulled the trigger. The Colt was empty. "Damn!" Marsh mounted the stallion, jerked its head to the left, dug spurs deep into its flanks and rode out. Upstairs, Lee Morgan realized he'd delayed too long to stop Marsh Coltrane. He'd have to do it the hard way. First, he'd make certain that Charity would stay put.

"Far enough, Morgan." He turned. Charity was on her feet—her forty-five leveled at Morgan's belly. "You've seen me shoot. You want to draw against a drop?"

"You've already used up your good luck and a sizeable share of somebody else's, Charity. Give it up. You're a woman. A young woman. They won't hang you."

"What then? Twenty years? Twenty-five? No, Morgan. That's too long for Charity Coltrane."

"It's not as long as dead!"

"Charity!" The beautiful, sensuous, deadly, greedy, misguided Charity Coltrane turned. There at the foot of the stairs stood Lucy Masters. She drew against the drop. The slug smashed into Charity's sternum—the breastbone—deflected into an oblique trajectory, ripping away the top of one lung and imbedding itself in Charity's spine. Still, Charity fired. The bullet buried itself in a far wall. Charity didn't know it. She was already dead.

Morgan looked down. His expression was blank. He hadn't had time to register a feeling about Lucy's defiance. When his mind finally conjured up a thought about it, he grinned. His thought was what she must have done to escape Pancho Villa's company.

"Get after Marsh. He rode south. Be careful." Morgan was already passing her. He nodded. "Morgan.

"Wait!" He frowned. He turned. "I told Villa he'd have to kill me to keep me there." She stopped.

"Yeah," Morgan said, tentatively.

"He rode back here with me." She didn't have to draw Morgan a picture.

"He saw Marsh ride out?" She nodded. "He's after him?" She nodded.

"I'll be careful," Morgan said.

Marsh Coltrane got a quarter of an hour's start on Pancho Villa, perhaps ten minutes more on Lee Morgan. The big, black stallion added to his edge. Villa's horse was a squatty animal, bred in Mexico for the *vaqueros* whose jobs often took them into rough terrain. She was the mare he used on the battlefield, not the thoroughbred he rode when he was desirous to impress someone.

Inside an hour, Villa was reduced to tracking Marsh's trail. Marsh rode almost due south out of the Double C ranch. The tracks stopped at the Frio River. Villa guessed Marsh would head for Mexico. If he stayed in the river, his speed would be cut and he would cut into the stage road about twelve miles northeast of Eagle Pass. Villa decided to gamble. He pushed the little pony hard, south to the stage road and then all out toward the border town. If Marsh once crossed into Mexico, it was a pure crap shoot as to which direction he would take. Villa had friends in Piedras Negras, just across the border. There, he could get a faster horse and, perhaps, some information.

Lee Morgan had an edge of his own. Young Jimmy Willow had overheard two of his guards discussing the possibility of a double-cross from Marsh Coltrane if plans went awry. One of them had said he'd run Marsh all the way to hell if he had to. But more likely, the gunhand said, he'd find Coltrane in the Mexican village of Hildago. Morgan opted to take his crap shoot up front.

Hildago, Coahila province, Mexico, was, in Lee Morgan's humble opinion, the world's rectum. A mile and a half west of the Rio Grande, it was a haven for whores, half-wits, men with no scruples and no country and a variety of crawling vermin which was much more preferable than its human inhabitants. A reasonably decent man who rode into Hildago and came out alive was, Morgan thought, a good candidate for his country's highest award for valor.

Morgan didn't hurry himself to get to Hildago. If he was right about Coltrane, the man would be there, taking stock of what he no longer commanded. If Morgan was wrong, it would make no difference. On the second morning after he rode away from the Double C, Morgan rode into Hildago. He reined up in front of the *Agua Negra cantina,* the Black Water saloon. He'd been told once that a visitor to Hildago could drink any liquid available in the village—including his own waste —and it would taste better than the water.

Morgan dismounted and immediately loaded the sixth

chamber on his revolver. He was already the subject of considerable scrutiny by a variety of Hildago vermin. He eyed both the spectators of his arrival and the surrounding terrain. It was a miserable collection of both. The one thing he didn't want at this point was any gunplay. He wasn't sure he could avoid it, but he intended to try. Just before he entered the *Agua Negra cantina,* Morgan loosed the tie on his black snake whip.

Morgan's thoughts were centered on the language. Inside the cantina, however, he spotted a grimy looking, overweight, underbathed, white man.

"Looking for a *yanqui.* Name's Coltrane. Marsh Coltrane. Would have ridden in on a big, black stallion. One—mebbe two days ago. You seen him?"

The man barely looked up from his fixation on a beetle which was struggling to right itself. Morgan waited. The man finally reached down and flipped the insect onto its feet. It scurried off in the direction of the bar. It was halfway there when the man produced one of two throwing knives from a waist belt, aimed and let go. He severed the beetle in half. He looked up—past Morgan.

"That's another drink you owe me," the fat man said. He got up, waddled to the knife and struggled to bend over and pick it up. He returned to the table. He sat down, poured a drink, downed it and wiped his mouth.

"I'll ask you again," Morgan said, "have you seen a *yanqui?*"

The fat man looked up. "You get pushy fast, don't you, friend?" Morgan sensed the trouble he'd walked into and decided then and there to face it down. He knew it would be tested at some point. He thought: why not now?

"Tell you what," Morgan said. "I'll stand you to what that gent owes you. Throw in a bottle of my own and buy the one you've already got against an answer to my question."

"Doing what?"

"Killing a beetle."

The man laughed. Others in the *cantina* laughed. The man asked, "What will you use, *gringo*," the man looked down, "the fancy boots you wear?"

"I'll give you another six feet of distance. We'll use the same beetle. I'll stop your knife in mid flight and kill the beetle."

The man stopped laughing. So did the others. He considered the young blond American. He eyed Morgan's six-gun. He stood up. He was a head taller than Morgan and his girth was double. Morgan tensed—ready.

"You're a liar, *gringo*."

"Prove it," Morgan said.

A little Mexican with a droopy moustache hurried from the bar, hands cupped. He opened them, revealing a large beetle. The fat man drew one of his knives, walked off six paces, somewhat more than six feet, scratched a mark into the rotten wood and walked back. He took the beetle, placed it on its back and then sat down. "Behind the line, *gringo*." Morgan moved to the line and turned. The man laughed and nodded to the little Mexican. In turn, he knelt down and flipped the beetle onto its back. It scurried toward the bar.

Morgan's right arm, still sore and stiff from his wound, nonetheless tensed. Blood surged through it into his fingers. Mentally, Morgan sent messages to the arm, messages he had sent scores of times. Messages which had never yet failed him.

The knife was drawn, delicately balanced for the

smallest part of a second and then spun, a turn and a half, toward its target. Morgan's arm was a flash of motion, a blur detected by only the sharpest of onlookers. The pistol barked, the knife shattered, the barrel moved like wheat in the wind, the pistol barked. The beetle vanished. The pistol dropped into the holster.

"I repeat, my fat friend," Morgan said, coolly, "have you seen a yanqui riding a black stallion?" The fat man's mouth was open but Morgan was watching his right hand. It had eased from the table's edge, moved to his knee, edged up toward his waist and a second throwing knife.

"He's back there," the fat man said, pointing with his left hand toward the rear of the *cantina*. At the same time he spoke and pointed, his right hand moved to his waist. Morgan killed him. Whirled and put two more shots over the head of the barkeep. The mirror, already cracked, flew from its frame. Three bottles were shattered and liquid and glassware showered those nearby.

"I get an answer now or someone has bought themselves my last shot."

"The *gringo* rode in two days ago, *señor*. He stays with Conchita Ruiz in adobe six miles south, *señor*. He waits for two *pistoleros* from Torreon. They come tomorrow. Maybe the next day."

"*Gracias, caballeros.*" Morgan backed from the *cantina*. He carefully checked the street in both directions and then mounted up. Slowly he backed his horse into the street and sidestepped the animals nearly half a block. Then, turning, he moved south with the horse at a canter.

The law in Hildago was simple. Survive. Morgan had —so far. A witness to his gun skill—a witness Morgan never saw, slipped out of the back door of the *Agua Negra cantina* and hurried along the backside of the dilapidated buildings. Inside an open barn which passed for the local livery stable, the witness, a boy of about sixteen, spoke to a surly, long-haired Mexican. The man, tall, slender and sporting a drooping moustache, smiled. He gave the boy five pesos.

A minute later, while Morgan was still backing out of the saloon, the man rode south—fast. He found Marsh Coltrane just saddling his horse.

"The *gringo* has come. He has killed *el cerdo*. He rides south." The man was smiling—a sinister smile. Marsh Coltrane knew this man would almost as soon see a contest between himself, Marsh, and the lightning fast *yanqui* as he would face the man himself for money. The choice was Marsh's.

"Three hundred dollars when you bring me the black snake whip he carried on his horse."

"I have heard of the *gringo's* speed, *señor*. I have dollars, *señor,* and I will bring the whip. But only to beetle in a single move. One thousand dollars, American dollars, *señor* and I will bring the whip. But only to show you. I keep it."

"I have friends coming," Marsh said. "Americans with guns too fast for his or yours. Perhaps I should pay them. Perhaps I will have two jobs for them."

The sinister man smiled. He eyed the window of the adobe. He could see no one, but he knew Conchita was there with a shotgun. "Perhaps, *señor,* but perhaps the *yanqui* will get here first. Perhaps your friends will come only to be at your funeral."

"Four hundred," Marsh said, "and the whip and whatever else he carries."

"Half now, *señor.*"

"Half now. You do it now on the trail between here and Hildago."

"As you wish, *señor* Coltrane." The man took the money, counted it, smiled, loaded his rifle, waved and rode off. He was barely out of sight when Marsh, joined by Conchita Ruiz, a Mexican prostitute of no more than eighteen years, mounted up and rode away from the adobe. Once again he rode south.

The Mexican gunman pulled his *sombrero* low over his eyes and slumped forward in the saddle. He gave the appearance of being drunk. He had covered nearly half the distance back to Hildago and had not encountered Lee Morgan. He had peered, carefully, from beneath his hat several times. He saw no signs of life. He cursed to himself. The *gringo* must have changed his mind or decided to wait in town for Coltrane to show. The Mexican stopped, shoved his hat back and stood up in his stirrups. Slowly, he scanned—one hundred eighty degrees. There was no rider.

The Mexican turned his horse and rode, fast, back to the adobe. He dismounted almost before the horse had come to a stop. He was barely off the animal when he looked up at the door of the crumbling building.

"You happen to be looking for me, *señor?*"

"*Madre de Dios!*"

The Mexican drew.

The Mexican died.

Morgan was still on a crap shoot. He was continuing to make his point. South of Hildago—so said the natives—there were two places a man could go. Hell or Laredo. If they didn't want trouble, most chose hell.

Morgan wanted Marshall Coltrane. Trouble now or trouble later. Morgan wanted it done. He chose Laredo.

The Mexican side of the Rio Grande, showing rather typical lack of imagination, was dubbed *Nuevo Laredo*. Morgan passed through this collection of whorehouses and *cantinas*. Laredo had plenty of both, but it was also a gathering point for wealthy Mexican and American businessmeen. The business, mostly, was stock. Sometimes cows, sometimes horses—usually less than above board. These businessmen didn't ask questions, rarely provided answers and had their own brand of dealing with interlopers.

Morgan hadn't been surprised to learn that Coltrane had been waiting for two gunmen. He'd been right, however, when he determined that Hildago was not the rendezvous point. The adobe had been no more than Marsh Coltrane's Mexican bank. Along with the ten thousand he'd taken from the Double C, Marsh had stashed quite a cache in Mexico in the preceding months. He'd stopped to pick it—and Conchita Ruiz up.

Morgan knew he must do what he had come to do quickly. Aside from the two gunmen Marsh was lining up, he'd have new contacts to make. Morgan had to strike first and now that would be tougher. Exactly three times tougher.

14

Morgan read the sign: *La Mujer de Oro—Cantina*.

It appealed to him. The Golden Lady saloon. He tied his horse at the single remaining spot at the hitching rail. It was summer. The peak of herding time. Friday night before many big drives north began. There would be buyers and sellers in Laredo—of almost anything.

The Golden Lady was not a sham. Its interior was an elegant display of someone's good taste. The bar, a dark, rich mahogany, ran the full length of the building —nearly half a block! The brass rail along its base was broken in continuity only by the placement of highly polished spitoons.

Saloon girls abounded. They and the male employees wore black toreador dress, save for the men's vest of gold brocade. He noted half a dozen men, posted at strategic positions, armed with shoulder rigs and shotguns. Fully half of the interior was devoted to gaming tables. There was no shortage of customers.

"Yes sir?"

"Whiskey."

"Our house whiskey is Kentucky Moon sir, unless

you have a preference.''

"That's fine.''

Morgan downed three shots. When the barkeep returned, Morgan asked, "I'm looking for a business associate. American. Tall. Dark haired. His name is Marshall Coltrane.''

"I'm sorry, sir, I rarely learn the names of our customers. Perhaps the house manager could be of service.'' The barkeep pointed. Morgan looked. This man was Mexican but wearing an American suit. Finely tailored. A telltale bulge under his left arm told Morgan he was more than just a manager.

"Thanks.''

"His name is Ramon Ortega.''

Morgan nodded and the barkeep walked away. It was then just Morgan's eyes met those of the girl. She was very tall with raven hair which hung to her waist. Her black eyes flashed in the bright lights of the cantina. She wore a fitted gown with a flared bottom and a bodice which both issued an invitation and made a promise. Their eyes locked. The girl moved her left hand. It held a fan. She moved the fan over her face, just below her eyes. She held it there for only a moment and then lowered it. Morgan knew the signal. The Mexican woman who had once served his father at the Spade Bit Ranch had explained them all. He didn't remember all of them. He remembered this one.

"Buenos noches, señorita.''

"Good evening,'' she said. She stood up. "Will you join me for a drink, *señor?''* Her eyes rolled toward the stairway. Morgan nodded, almost unnoticibly.

The room was as immaculate, if not as large, as the casino. The woman went immediately to a credenza.

She didn't turn when she asked, "What is your desire, *señor*?" It wasn't a drink but that was a starting point.

"Whiskey."

"I have some excellent American stock, a Tennessee blend, I believe."

"Fine." She poured two and brought Morgan his.

"To us, *señor.*" They drank. She gestured toward two chairs at a small table in the corner. "You think me brash?"

"I think you're a very beautiful woman with an excellent command of my language and," Morgan looked around, "equally excellent tastes."

"But not too forward?"

"I'm not much on small talk, although I do like to know just who it is I'm talking to."

"They call me Hermosa."

"Beautiful. It fits."

"And you?"

"Lee Morgan."

"A buyer or seller of cattle? Or horses?"

"Neither. I'm looking for a man. An American."

"Then you are a lawman?"

"Not that either. Or a bounty hunter or a killer. I work for someone in Texas who was wronged by this man. I'd like to take him back to face my employer."

"Must you find this man tonight?"

"No."

"Then, *señor* Morgan, will you stay with me?"

Morgan got to his feet. "Don't be insulted. But no, I won't."

"Do you think me a prostitute?"

"No. At least that is not the impression you've given."

"I am not. So money can't be your reason." Morgan thought: I've got no good reason, and I'll think of myself as a damned fool later. His eyes traveled to the cleavage. The breathing only added to the desire as the woman's breasts rose and fell almost like a heartbeat.

"I've been on the trail for nearly four days. I'm damned roady. I'm even more tired. I couldn't do either of us justice."

Hermosa smiled. "I've never met a man who cared about how well he performed—or that the woman received any enjoyment at all."

Morgan's eyes had just shifted from the cleavage again when they caught sight of a dark, moving patch on the sloped side of one of the glasses. He twisted, dropped, rolled behind a love seat and heard the muffled scream as the bullet tore into Hermosa's lovely, undulating left breast. The manager's gaze froze on the woman's body. His mouth dropped open in the shock of what he'd done. Morgan killed him. The man behind him ran. Morgan had already gauged the outside front of the building. The fancy sign hung from a low, sloping roof. Access to the roof could be gained from one of six windows. He was right by one of them. He got to the roof without opening the window.

Morgan ran to the end of the roof, sat down with his feet and legs dangling over the edge, twisted, grabbing the edge and then dropping. He landed, knees bent, but upright. The man behind the manager burst through the bat wing doors. He might have saved his life if he'd kept moving. Down and in between the horses, he stopped. He looked left. He looked right. He died.

A rider galloped by, hell bent for leather. He fired twice. One bullet took Morgan's hat off and he felt the scrape against the flesh. Too close! Too goddam close. Morgan got off two shots. The man was too low in the saddle and moving too fast.

By the time Morgan had reached his own horse, the rider was out of sight, having turned the corner a block away. Morgan dug his spurs into his mount and the animal responded by throwing divots of street with her rear hooves. Morgan turned the corner. There was no sign of the rider. Morgan reined up.

Man and horse burst into view behind a fusillade of pistol fire from between two buildings. Morgan's horse whinnied. She was hit. He dismounted, slipping the Winchester into his arms as he did so. He came up from the crouch, aimed, levered, fired and saw the rider stiffen in the saddle and then tumble from it. The horse turned, slipped, and then bolted into the darkness.

If Marsh Coltrane had accomplished anything at all for himself it was limited to having bought a little more time. Morgan had gained much more from the experience. He cussed himself a score of times for having been so damned predictable. It could have caused him a very serious breathing problem!

In the daylight, *La Mujer de Oro* suddenly looked like any other whorehouse and saloon Morgan had ever been in—with just a touch more class. In daylight, the two gunnies, both Mexican, proved to be locals with more greed than skills. In daylight, Laredo was a hot, dusty, miserable Texas border town with a mean reputation and too damned many people to make it easy to find one.

Morgan was low on funds. Something he hadn't thought about when he rode out of the Double C. He was in need of a horse and some ammunition. He managed both, but there would be no rooms better than the good old *La Cucaracha* back in Uvalde.

One thing daylight did do in Laredo. It loosened some tongues. By noon, Morgan had learned from three of the Golden Lady girls and two waiters, with some encouragement from his six-gun, that the American and two mean types had spent most of an afternoon in the place. The reason for their visit and its results—were now obvious. One of the girls, however, put Morgan on a trail which, if he didn't act quickly, would grow cold fast.

There was a minor rail spur running north and east out of Laredo. Three men had stolen a hand car, blocked the rails about ten miles out, halted and robbed an incoming train. It was a payroll train which carried cattle sellers' money to the Laredo bank. The American and his two friends in the Golden Lady were overheard stating that they had to meet three friends in four days at rail terminal called Pescadito Junction.

Morgan rode out of Laredo.

And now there were six.

Pescadito Junction was a water tower, a one room railroad agent's shack, a two story whorehouse and saloon and a barn with half a roof. The latter served as the local livery. Morgan arrived at the barn at midday. The heat was stifling. There was not so much as a ripple in the air to stir a leaf had there been a tree nearby. There wasn't.

"Buenos dias señor." The man at the livery barn was shirtless. Sweat poured from a balding head, ran in rivulets along every wrinkle in his face, dripped from his chin and onto a dirty, hairy chest. There, it disappeared

—maybe, Morgan thought, drowning some lice. The man was barefooted. The big toe on his left foot was black—infected from the look of it. The man couldn't see it. His gut blocked the view. "You wish me to care for your horse?"

"Can you handle a seventh?" The man looked surprised. "You do have six others here, don't you?"

"*Si!*"

"I'll keep mine. Thanks just the same. Now about the men who own the other six. Are they all in the saloon?" The fat man's eyes shifted toward the one room railroad agent's shack. Quickly. They shifted back. He smiled.

"*Si, señor.*"

"Yeah. Now, my friend, if you've lied to me, I'll come back in a few minutes and I'll kill you. One more time. Are all the men at the saloon?" The fat man swallowed.

"I theenk, *señor—uno*—one maybe—there." He pointed to the agent's shack.

"And the others?"

The man shrugged. "I cannot say for sure." He smiled. A weak smile.

"Try saying unsure." Morgan loosed the strap holding his black snake whip in place. The fat man swallowed.

"Two upstairs. Three down."

"The one in the agent's shack. Why?"

"*Dinamita!*" He gestured with both hands, indicating an explosion. "*Estampido. Estampido.*"

"They're planning to blow up a train!"

"*Si, si.* Blow up. *Si, si.*"

"With dynamite?" The man nodded. Pleased, it seemed, that Morgan both understood and believed.

Morgan was, in fact, puzzled. What train? Why? If he'd heard right, they'd already hit the payroll train. They had ridden to Pescadito just to split up the loot.

"What train?"

"Federales, señor, they come soon. *Hoy."*

"Today."

"Si." The man looked concerned, rubbed his facial stubble in thought, trying to come up with some reasonable English. *"El tren,* she *transporter.* She carries *armas para el revolucion."*

"Jeezus! Guns! Weapons for the revolution."

"Si si! El revolucion de Pancho Villa."

Morgan considered the fat man at the livery barn, but his mind was back-tracking to San Antonio. He remembered! A little map—hand drawn. It didn't amount to much. A railroad line—isolated. An X at one end. The letters P S at the other. The map was in a most unlikely place. The bedroom of Madiera Lucia de Lopez! Morgan hadn't payed much mind to it. After all, he was about to bed the bitch.

Everything came home. Morgan remembered that de Lopez had told him it was Madiera's idea to engage the little freight line from Uvalde. *Inconspicuous* she'd called it. Inconspicuous in a pig's ass! The Masters Cartage Company of Uvalde, Texas was a goddam decoy. Everything Villa did and planned was being shunted right straight to his enemies. Via de Lopez's beautiful, totally unprincipled daughter!

Marsh Coltrane's payoff would have been double. He makes a deal to keep the attention away from the actual weapons shipment. He stages raids, attacks the freight wagons, burns ranches and, in general, raises hell. Everybody is looking for him. When it's over and done,

Marsh has the Double C ranch as well as the payroll train's loot because he's tipped to when and where he can hit it and, more than likely, Madiera de Lopez.

"Gracias," Morgan said. The man frowned, thinking Morgan looked strange suddenly. Preoccupied. Distant, in mind at least. The man couldn't know just how right he was. Morgan dismounted, pulled his whip and his Winchester from the horse. "Stall her." The fat man nodded. He'd no doubt been subjected to similar fear when Marsh and his gunnies rode in. The poor bastard was caught between a rock and a hard place. He had no loyalties except to himself. No goals except staying alive. There were hundreds—indeed thousands in Mexico in the same fix. In trying to change it, Pancho Villa was a hero. How much of the exposure to power would taint Villa's efforts was not for Morgan to judge. History would do that. Long after both he and Villa were supporting marble headstones. Now was now. Villa was the lesser of two evils.

A hundred yards separated the livery barn from the agent's shanty. Morgan had covered about half of it when the lone occupant of the shack appeared in the doorway. Morgan had not seen the man before. The man had not seen Morgan before. Both knew why the other was there. The man was fast—very fast. He wasn't accurate or, if so, he didn't take his time. Morgan did. And now there were five.

The exchange of shots brought predictable results. Two men charged out of the saloon. Morgan charged into the railroad shack. He spotted the plunger. He cut the wires. Bullets began ripping through the rotten wood of the building and what was left of the windows. Morgan went through one of them—on the backside.

He crossed the tracks and dropped behind the roadbed—Winchester at the ready.

There were more shots. They seemed restricted to the saloon. Someone had no doubt gotten in the way. Either that or Marsh Coltrane was displaying another fit of temper. Morgan cocked his head. Boots scraping against loose stones. Morgan rolled away from the tracks. A man appeared off to his left. The man fired. He missed. Morgan fired. He missed. He moved back toward the shack.

Half a block away, Marsh Coltrane stood outside the saloon with two men. Both white men. Both wearing two guns. Both highly skilled at using them. Toby Stiles was twenty-eight. He'd killed at least eight men in gunfights, two of them lawmen. Dave Eubanks was forty. No one was certain how many men he'd killed. But he hadn't faced all of them. Honor was not part of Dave's make-up.

"I'll send the Mexicans toward the shanty. One for each side. Morgan either shows himself or dies. If he showes himself, you be ready."

"Lemme call him out," Toby said.

"Do as you're told, Stiles. You don't know Lee Morgan." Marsh looked at his pocket watch. "Besides, we haven't the time for fancy gunplay. That train will reach the dynamite in another twenty minutes. We've got to have that shack back before that."

Toby Stiles scowled. He didn't need to know Lee Morgan. He knew Toby Stiles, and he knew he could beat anybody. He watched as Dave Eubanks talked to the Mexicans. They protested at first, but Dave told them something and one of them started in a long loop around the saloon to get to the far side of the railroad shack.

Morgan, for his part, was still trying to piece together the sudden influx of information. He was thinking about what the fat man said. *Federales*. Government soldiers. They would be here today. Why? Someone—Villa perhaps—had to pick up the weapons. An ambush. Had Villa known all along? Morgan concluded that at least Villa knew of Marsh Coltrane's plans or enough of them to want to get Marsh.

In fact, Morgan concluded, Villa's passion for wanting Marsh Coltrane wasn't a passion to kill him—but to protect him. To keep Morgan from killing him until Villa could find out what he was up to. Morgan shook his head. He could have reasoned much of this out earlier—way earlier. Maybe a few people would still be alive if he had. He heard boots in the gravel.

Morgan had completely shifted position. He'd crawled on his belly away from the shack, over the railroad bed, and along it for some twenty-five yards. He was now almost parallel with one of the Mexicans who was closing on the shack.

"*Aqui,*" Morgan shouted. The Mexican turned. Morgan killed him. He dropped into a prone position, used the roadbed for an elbow and barrel rest, tightened his grip on the Winchester, sighted in on the second Mexican who was now running away from him, judged the distance at about ninety yards and fired!

Now there were three.

Face *me* you sonuvabitch!" Toby Stiles started walking toward the shack. Dave Eubanks started to stop him. Marsh stopped Eubanks.

"Let the kid die. Get to the livery. Get a horse. Get

215

down to the dynamite. Stay there and blow it with a rifle shot.''

"And you, Coltrane? You ridin' out with the payroll money?''

"I'll meet you, Dave. South. One day. Hell. It'll be just you and me.''

"Uh uhn. If Toby dies, it'll be you, me an' Morgan. We stay 'til he dies.''

Every man there heard the rider—a lone rider—coming in full bore. Morgan saw him first. He wore the uniform of a Mexican *Federale*. He rode in from the south. The sudden appearance distracted Toby Stiles. Morgan put the Winchester down.

"Stiles!" Eighty-four feet separated the men. Stiles wore a Colt's .45 Peacemaker low on his right leg. Too damned low. Still, he was greased lightning. He was no more than a tenth of a second behind Morgan's draw. But he was about two inches less accurate at that distance. He died wondering what the hell went wrong.

The *Federale* lost his footing when he dismounted. The horse kept going. The *Federale* barked Spanish too fast for either man—Marsh or Dave Eubanks. Marsh started trying to settle the man down.

"Get him, Dave. Kill Morgan. I don't care how. Kill him!'' Dave considered Marsh Coltrane. He grinned and shook his head. He knew what one man, determined and skilled, could do against numbers. The lone man had nothing to lose. Every success reduced the odds and unravelled a few more nerves in his adversary. Eubanks had been there. He'd been the lone stalker. He'd also just seen a display of speed and accuracy which he knew he couldn't match.

He darted for the saloon. Marsh grabbed the Mexican

and pulled him inside as well. Morgan looked around and picked his next move. Inside the saloon, Marsh Coltrane listened to the Mexican soldier. His force, twenty-five men, had been ambushed. Forty riders, many armed with only clubs, but vicious and unafraid and led by none other than Pancho Villa himself. The plans had gone awry again.

In a typical display of a second rate leader who finally recognizes that he has lost, Marsh Coltrane killed the messenger for the message he delivered. He'd seen Dave Eubanks go upstairs. He smiled. It was time to get the hell out of Pescadito Junction. He headed for the back door.

Dave Eubanks, a high-powered Winchester fitted with a telescopic sight in his hands, peered from the saloon window. He spotted Lee Morgan's hat crown just above the edge of the railroad shack's window. He smiled. He aimed, lowering the barrel and knowing full well the bullet's capacity for piercing the two by four frame. He fired. The hat disappeared.

"Up here!" Eubanks' eyes got big and round. He leaned out, looking up and to the left toward the sound. It came from the top of the water tower. Morgan fired. Now there was one.

Pancho Villa stepped out of the livery barn. Marsh Coltrane froze in his tracks. Villa drew both his pistols, firing them alternately. Marsh, no slouch in a pinch, dived, rolled, drew and fired three times. It was all he could fire. His gun was empty. It was all he had to fire. He hit Villa in the leg. He charged the Mexican bandit, kicked the guns from his hands, and a bullet tore up the dirt near him. He turned. Morgan was coming. Marsh bolted.

Inside the livery, he backed the big, black stallion out
of the stall, mounted up, spurred the animal and tore
out of the barn, wheeled and rode east. Morgan knelt by
Villa.

"Everything you were doing was being—" Villa was
shaking his head and smiling.

"I know, *señor* Morgan." He gestured with his head.
"Get Coltrane. Now you can get him, *señor*. I don't
need him anymore."

"I can't catch him. Not with my mount."

"He's riding toward my men, *señor*. He will have to
turn back. He has no *pistola*. Get him, Morgan."

A breeze now blew across the open country from
south to north. It didn't cool things down. The wind
was hot. The dust devils danced on the desert floor. The
heat of the midday sun struck and ground and bounced
off creating opaque, wavering barriers through which
everything appeared distorted.

Morgan saw the line of riders. They appeared more
distant than they were. Their horses legs looked rubbery
and twisted through the heat waves. Between him and
the riders, there was Marshall Coltrane.

He saw the riders. He reined up. He looked south.
There were more. He looked north. The train was
coming in. He turned his horse. He saw Lee Morgan.
He spurred the black stallion, rode forward about fifty
yards, unsheathed his rifle and held it in the air. Morgan
reined up. Marsh wanted out. Morgan didn't mind
obliging him.

Marsh looped the reins around the saddle horn,

leaving a little slack. The stallion pawed, seemingly aware of the imminent charge. Morgan wet his lips, tucked the reins in his mouth and bit down. He hefted the Winchester out of its scabbard. He checked it for load and levered a shell into the chamber.

Marsh Coltrane spurred the stallion and he dropped his rump, dug in and plowed forward. Morgan waited. The stallion picked up speed. Marsh leaned forward in the saddle, bringing the rifle to bear. Morgan waited. Marsh fired. Morgan heard the shell. Morgan spurred his horse.

Marsh Coltrane lifted the rifle across in front of his body to work the lever action. He'd fired the first time one handed. Morgan used both as though he was stationary. Holding reins in his mouth, he tugged or released pressure on them to signal his mount for the slightest movement. Marsh fired. Morgan winced and grunted. The bullet tore through his boot top and cut a ridge of flesh away from the inside part of his left ankle.

Morgan fired. The bullet struck Marsh's right thigh, dead center. It burrowed through tissue, muscle and finally imbedded itself in the femur. Marsh brought up his rifle to work the lever. Morgan fired. The second shot struck the saddle horn. It ripped the horn away, the reins dropped, the bullet split and a section of it buried itself in Marsh Coltrane's groin. He screamed. He dropped his weapon.

The loop in the reins dropped to the ground, the stallion's foreleg stepped through it, the animal's eyes turned fiery red in fear. It struggled to stay on its feet. It did. Marsh Coltrane, his hands cupped over his groin, went forward over the horse's head. He could not control his movement or break his fall in time. He was

in a semi-ball and landed almost on the top of his head.
Weight and momentum combined to break his neck. He
lived for another full minute.

15

Madiera Lucia de Lopez tried to flee to Mexico. There, she would have married the son of *El Presidente*. Villa's men caught her. The beautiful Madiera would have ended her own life but for one man. Her father. He shot her through the heart.

Lee Morgan collected his money. A considerable sum from all sources. He bought a new horse, new trail gear, and new clothes. He stayed at the Double C ranch. It now belonged to Lucy Masters, purchased at auction when the county established that there were no family members to take it over. It reverted to the state for taxes.

Morgan was ready to ride out to Mexico. He still had a year of servitude and a few gun hands to round up. Villa had kept his word. Now Morgan would have to keep his.

"*Ahh. Señor Morgan. Mi Amigo.*" Morgan was just exiting the ranch house. He looked up and saw Pancho Villa. He was mounted on Marsh Coltrane's black stallion.

"You already own a black horse, Villa. Why do you want another one?"

"One for battle. One for the *parada. El grande exstasiar!*"

"Parade? Grand entrance. Into what?"

"Mehico City, mi amigo. When the lightning-fast *Yanqui* has killed all my enemies, I will ride in. *El Presidente."*

"You got a helluva vivid imagination, Villa," Morgan said.

Villa laughed. *"Si.* One day perhaps. But it is a long time yet."

"Well let's get to it."

"Manana, señor Morgan. Manana!"

"Bullshit on tomorrow. I've got nothing holding me here."

"Behind you, *mi amigo."* Morgan frowned and turned. There stood Lucy Masters. She was supposed to have been in El Paso.

"The *revolucion.* She will keep a day or two perhaps," Villa said.

"Or a week," Morgan said. He walked over to Lucy. "What the hell are you doing here?"

"Can I go to Mexico with you?"

"Absolutely not!"

"Then whatever we do will have to be done here, won't it?"

"Uh huh." Morgan turned. "A week, Villa. That's how long the revolution will have to keep. A week. You'll just have to find something to occupy yourself."

Villa laughed. "Perhaps a few days with my *prima."*

"Your *cousin?"*

"In *Mehico* a cousin is closer than a cousin in your

country.'' Villa motioned with his arm. A very young girl rode up beside him. "This is the girl of whom I spoke before, *señor* Morgan. She helped me find Coltrane and got from him the information of *señorita* de Lopez. This, *señor* Morgan, is Conchita Ruiz. *Mi prima!*''

"Well I'll be goddamned," Morgan said.